Richard Anthony Proctor

Easy Lessons in the Differential Calculus

Indicating from the outset the utility of the processes called

differentiation and integration. Third Edition

Richard Anthony Proctor

Easy Lessons in the Differential Calculus
Indicating from the outset the utility of the processes called differentiation and integration. Third Edition

ISBN/EAN: 9783337387815

Printed in Europe, USA, Canada, Australia, Japan

Cover: Foto ©Andreas Hilbeck / pixelio.de

More available books at **www.hansebooks.com**

THE

DIFFERENTIAL CALCULUS.

PRINTED BY

SPOTTISWOODE AND CO., NEW-STREET SQUARE

LONDON

EASY LESSONS

IN THE

DIFFERENTIAL CALCULUS:

INDICATING FROM THE OUTSET THE UTILITY OF
THE PROCESSES CALLED

DIFFERENTIATION AND INTEGRATION.

BY

RICHARD A. PROCTOR,

AUTHOR OF 'CHANCE AND LUCK,' 'FIRST STEPS IN GEOMETRY,'
'THE GEOMETRY OF CYCLOIDS,' AND THE ARTICLES ON
ASTRONOMY IN THE 'ENCYCLOPÆDIA BRITANNICA'
AND THE 'AMERICAN CYCLOPÆDIA.'

'Most excellent differences.'—Shakespeare.

THIRD EDITION.

LONDON:

LONGMANS, GREEN, AND CO.

AND NEW YORK : 15 EAST 16th STREET.

1889.

PREFACE.

I FIRST took interest in algebra when I found that problems in Single and Double Position could be solved much more readily by algebra than by the rather absurd rules given for such problems in books on arithmetic. In like manner, I could find no interest in the Differential Calculus till, after wading through two hundred pages of matter having no apparent use (and for the most part really useless), I found the calculus available for the ready solution of problems in Maxima and Minima. This little work has been planned with direct reference to my own experience at school and college. The usual method of teaching the Differential and Integral Calculus seems to me almost as absurd (quite as absurd it could scarcely be) as the plan by which children, instead of being taught how to speak—whether their own language or another—are made to learn by rote rules relating to the philosophy of language such as not one grammarian in ten thousand ever thinks about in after life.

I have striven in this little work (reprinted here from the pages of KNOWLEDGE) to show at once how and why we want a method of calculation dealing with quantities which vary in value under various conditions, and how such a method of calculation is to be used in practice.

The Integral Calculus I have treated as simply a department of the Differential Calculus, dealing with it in the same practical manner.

It may interest learners to know that, chancing when at Cambridge to be my own master, with freedom to choose what I would learn, I took up for my degree rather less of the Differential Calculus than is presented for beginners here. What I have had occasion to study since respecting the Differential Calculus, the Calculus of Variations and higher matter, I have dealt with as occasion required—the only really effective way of studying mathematics.

RICHARD A. PROCTOR.

ST. JOSEPH MO.:
    May 1887.

CONTENTS.

———•◦•———

Errata.

Page 3, line 8, *for* be described as the rate with which the space it has *read* be described as the rate at which the space it has

„   4,   „   3, for $\frac{1}{2}g(t+1)^2-gt^2$ read $\frac{1}{2}g(t+1)^2-\frac{1}{2}gt^2$

„   „   lines 21, 22, *for* fallen in t seconds $-\frac{1}{2}gt^2$ *read* fallen in t seconds $=\frac{1}{2}gt^2$

„ 15, line 7, *for* In other words, from our knowledge that $\frac{gt}{2}$ is *read* In other words, from our knowledge that $\frac{gt^2}{2}$ is

„ 51, „   6, *for* $9 = \dfrac{\sqrt{9+x^2}}{4}+\dfrac{5-x}{5}$ *read* $y=\dfrac{\sqrt{9+x^2}}{4}+\dfrac{5-x}{5}$

„ 56, „   5, *for* $< \dfrac{h}{2x(x-h)}$ *read* which last-mentioned expression $= \dfrac{h}{2x(x-h)}$

„ 90, „ 11, *for* $\sqrt{2ax-x^2}=x\sqrt{1-z^2}$; *read* $\sqrt{2ax-a^2}=x\sqrt{1-z^2}$;

„   „   „ 12, *for* $\therefore \displaystyle\int \frac{dx}{x\sqrt{2ax-x^2}}=$ &c. *read* $\therefore \displaystyle\int \frac{dx}{x\sqrt{2ax-a^2}}=$ &c.

„ 95, „   1, *for* the triangle QOP$=$OP.OQ sin QOP *read* the triangle QOP$=\frac{1}{2}$OP.OQ sin QOP.

„   „   „ 10, *for* Sector AOB$=\frac{1}{2}\displaystyle\int_0^a r^2d\theta=\frac{r^2}{2}\displaystyle\int^a d\theta$ *read* Sector AOB$=\frac{1}{2}\displaystyle\int_0^a r^2d\theta=\frac{r^2}{2}\displaystyle\int_0^a d\theta.$

Page 96, line 4, *for* product of the radius and the circumfe-rence. But *read* product of one-half the radius and the circumference.

„ 103, „ 21, *for* Then $CA = a$ and $CG = \sqrt{2a} =$ &c. *read* Then $CA = a$ and $CG = \dfrac{a}{\sqrt{2}} =$ &c.

„ 105, „ 12, *for* $CN = Nn' = \dfrac{Cn}{\sqrt{2}}$ *read* $CN = Nn' = \dfrac{Cn'}{\sqrt{2}}$

„ „ „ 14, *for* $= \dfrac{CN' + N'K}{a} = \dfrac{x_1 + \sqrt{x_2^2 - a^2}}{a}$ *read* $\dfrac{CN' + N'K}{a} = \dfrac{x_1 + \sqrt{x_1^2 - a^2}}{a}$

„ 109, „ 5, *for* Whence, differentiating $2xz + x^2$ with respect to z, *read* **Whence,** differentiating $2xz - z^2$ with respect to z.

„ 110, „ 7, *for* $\displaystyle\int \sqrt{x^2 - a^2}\,dx = \dfrac{x\sqrt{a^2 - a^2}}{2} -$ &c. *read* $\displaystyle\int \sqrt{x^2 - a^2}\,dx = \dfrac{x\sqrt{x^2 - a^2}}{2} -$ &c.

„ „ in line 16, *for* Fig. 22. *read* Fig. 23.

EASY LESSONS

DIFFERENTIAL CALCULUS.

———◆◇◆———

LESSON I.

PURPOSE OF THE DIFFERENTIAL CALCULUS.

THE Differential Calculus is the science which deals with the rate at which variable quantities increase or diminish. When we say that a quantity is variable, we imply that it varies as some other quantity changes. For example, the velocity of a train is variable. It varies with the *time* which has elapsed since the train started—it varies with the *distance traversed*—with the *steam power* employed—with the *state of the rails*—and so on. But the differential calculus deals only with those quantities which vary according to some definite law.

For example, when a body is let fall from rest the distance it traverses varies, according to a known law, with the time elapsed since the fall began. The differential calculus is able to deal with such a case as this. Again, the sine of an angle varies according

B

to a known law as the angle changes; and the differential calculus is therefore able to deal with this case also.

Now we can at once see the importance of a calculus which will deal with variable quantities. Algebra and geometry and trigonometry deal with absolute quantities. But it is often very necessary to learn something about the variations of quantities, to know when a variable quantity attains its greatest value, when it is increasing, when diminishing, when it changes fastest, and so on. Whenever variations take place according to a known law, this is precisely what the differential calculus will do for us. And its great advantage is that it will solve our problems systematically. An ingenious application of algebra or geometry or trigonometry will often enable us to solve problems which belong especially to the differential calculus; but we require ingenuity for the purpose, whereas the differential calculus solves such problems with certainty, even if we have not a particle of ingenuity, so long only as we follow the proper rules. Even where it fails, it teaches us that we are trying to solve an insoluble problem.

The first matter the calculus attends to is the choice of a convenient expression for the rate at which a variable quantity changes. This expression is called a *differential coefficient.* I prefer to illustrate rather than to define it. I wish also to illustrate it in such a way as to remove at the outset the chief

stumbling block of the student of this special department of mathematics. I take, therefore, a familiar
case of a varying quantity :—

When a body is let fall from rest, we know that
as it falls its velocity continually increases. Now
this varying velocity affords a very good illustration of
a differential coefficient. The velocity of a body may
be described as the rate ~~with~~ which the space it has
traversed is increasing as the time elapsed increases.
When we change the time, we change the space
traversed. But unless the velocity is uniform, the
change of space is not proportional to the change of
time. In the case of a falling body, the velocity is
not uniform ; so that, if we consider one instant, the
rate at which the space traversed would change for
any given interval of time would be different from
the corresponding rate at some other instant. Regarding the matter as illustrating the differential
calculus, the first thing to be found is a general
expression for the rate of change—the law determining the space traversed being supposed known.

Consider now the following way of dealing with
the problem :—

At the end of t seconds the body has fallen a
space represented by $\frac{1}{2}gt^2$, where g represents the
accelerating force of gravity (or numerically, a foot
being taken as the unit of length, and a second as
the unit of time, $g = 32\cdot2$). A second later the
body has fallen altogether a space represented by

$$\tfrac{1}{2}g(t + 1)^2,$$

so that in the course of that second the space actually traversed by the body is

$$\tfrac{1}{2}g(t + 1)^2 - \tfrac{1}{2}gt^2$$
$$= gt + \frac{g}{2}.$$

And if during that second the body moved with uniform velocity, we should at once know what that velocity is. For, when a body moves uniformly over s units of length in t units of time, it moves over $\frac{s}{t}$ units of length in one unit of time, and $\frac{s}{t}$ therefore represents its velocity. So that the velocity of our falling body would be

$$\left(gt + \frac{g}{2}\right) \div 1$$

if the body had moved uniformly during the second. But this is not the case. The body moves faster and faster as the second of time is passing; and its velocity at time t is therefore *not* obtained by the above process. We should clearly get a better result if we took a shorter interval of time. Suppose we take a very short interval indeed, as a thousandth part of a second. Then we have, as before, the space fallen in t seconds

$$= \tfrac{1}{2}gt^2,$$

the space traversed one thousandth of a second later

$$= \tfrac{1}{2}g\left(t + \frac{1}{1000}\right)^2$$

and the space traversed in the interval

$$= \frac{gt}{1000} + \frac{g}{2(1000)^2}.$$

So that on the false supposition of uniform velocity during this minute interval, we get for this velocity,

$$\left[\frac{gt}{1000} + \frac{g}{2(1000)^2}\right] \div \frac{1}{1000},$$

or

$$\cdot gt + \frac{g}{2000}.$$

This is clearly nearer the truth, because in so short an interval as a thousandth part of a second the change of velocity is exceedingly minute. But still we have not the exact velocity.

If we had taken a yet smaller interval, as the millionth part of a second, we should have deduced for the velocity

$$gt + \frac{g}{2(1000000)},$$

which is yet nearer the truth.

And the minuter the interval, the minuter the second fraction becomes, the first remaining un-altered. Also, the minuter the interval, the nearer we get to the true value.

But there is nothing to prevent us from conceiving that the interval is taken infinitely minute, in which case the second fraction disappears, and also we get infinitely near to the true value. This value then is gt, and as a matter of fact we know independently that this is the velocity acquired by a falling body in the time t.

Now the reader will not need to be told that I have not gone through these processes merely for the sake of deducing this special result. I want him to convince himself of the reasonableness of the above method, and also I wish him to note that though the reasoning has introduced the conception of *infinitely minute quantities*, and though the result itself is a *limiting* value, yet that result is none the less *exact*. The velocity a body has at the end of any specified time is real, and not a mere mathematical fiction or approximation.

Prepared then to see that a real and exact value can be deduced by a seemingly approximate method, let him consider the following way of treating the same problem :—

Let s represent the space traversed in time t $s + \Delta s$ the space traversed in time $t + \Delta t$ (where Δs and Δt are to be looked upon as simple quantities, which may be read, if we please, *increment of the space* and *increment of the time*; or else, for convenience, simply *delta-space* and *delta-time*). Then

$$s = \tfrac{1}{2}gt^2 . \qquad . \quad . \quad . \quad . \text{(i.)}$$

$$s + \Delta s = \tfrac{1}{2}g(t + \Delta t)^2 \quad . \quad . \quad . \text{(ii.)}$$

and therefore, subtracting (i.) from (ii.),

$$\Delta s = gt\Delta t + \frac{g}{2}(\Delta t)^2$$

so that if the velocity of the body during the interval Δt were uniform, this velocity, or $\dfrac{\Delta s}{\Delta t}$, would

$$= gt + \frac{g}{2}\Delta t.$$

This result, however, will not be true, unless Δt is infinitely minute. Let Δt be supposed to be made infinitely minute, in which condition call it dt; then Δs also becomes infinitely minute, and (to indicate this condition) may be called ds; and we get

$$\frac{ds}{dt} = gt + \frac{g}{2}\,dt$$

$= gt$, since dt is infinitely minute or nought.

Now this quantity $\dfrac{ds}{dt}$, for which we have thus obtained a definite value (although ds and dt are each evanescent), is called *the differential coefficient of s* (the space traversed) *with respect to t* (the time). It is really *the rate at which the space is increasing at the time t.*

But the reader will presently have to consider differential coefficients in a general way. The above illustration has shown him how a differential coefficient is deduced in a special case; and also that a differential coefficient, though made up of seemingly evanescent parts, may have an exact value, and (what is yet more to the purpose) has *always a real* significance. The $\dfrac{ds}{dt}$ of our illustration is that real and

familiar relation, the velocity of a falling body.   And
so the differential coefficients **we have to** deal **with**
as **we** proceed, **are real** matters, not mathematical
fictions.

But the above case will serve as well to illustrate
the meaning **of** what is called *integration* as the
meaning **of** *differentiation*—the name given to the
process actually followed above.   **This** I proceed to
show in Lesson **II.**

LESSON II.

PURPOSE OF THE INTEGRAL CALCULUS.

ILLUSTRATING a *differential coefficient* by the case of a body falling under the action of the constant force of terrestrial gravity, g, we supposed the space (s) fallen through by a body in a given time (t) to be known —since for the purpose of our illustration it was not necessary to show how s is determined. But it so happens that, in taking this instance to illustrate the *integral* calculus, we have to consider how s is determined, from what, in reality, is all that is known in this case. We know that the force g being constant, the velocity generated in any time is proportional to the time, so that, if v be this velocity, we may write $v = gt$, suitable units of time and length being taken. (Usually the unit of time is a second, that of length a foot; in which case, $g = 32\cdot2$ and $v = 32\cdot2t$.)

Now, knowing that $v = gt$, we may try the same expedient to determine the space traversed at the end of any time t from rest, as we employed in the inverse problem. We may divide up the time into a number of small parts, and suppose the velocity uniform during each short interval of time. Let us see what comes of this experiment. Take $t = n\tau$, where τ is very small and therefore n very large. Then, at the beginning of the rth interval, the velocity is $(r-1)g\tau$, and at the end of this interval the velocity is $rg\tau$. Thus the space traversed in the interval lies between $(r-1)g\tau^2$ and $rg\tau^2$. Doing this for all the intervals, and adding, we find that the total space traversed in time $n\tau$ or t lies between

$$[0+1+2+3+\ldots+(r-1)+\ldots+(n-1)]g\tau^2$$

and

$$[1+2+3+\ldots\ldots+r \quad +\ldots+n]g\tau^2$$

that is, summing these arithmetical series, between

$$\frac{n(n-1)}{2}g\tau^2 \text{ and} \frac{n(n+1)}{2}g\tau^2;$$

or (writing for τ its equivalent $t \div n$) between

$$\frac{n^2-n}{2n^2}gt^2 \text{ and } \frac{n^2+n}{2n^2}gt^2$$

i.e. $\dfrac{gt^2}{2} - \dfrac{gt^2}{2n}$ and $\dfrac{gt^2}{2} + \dfrac{gt^2}{2n}$.

The larger n is, the smaller is the second term of each expression. But we may have n as large as we please, and so bring these two expressions as near to each other in value as we please. This means, of course, that the true value of each, when n is infinite, is

$$\frac{gt^2}{2}.$$

This, then, is the space traversed in time t by a falling body starting from rest, under the action of terrestrial gravity. That is, we have established the relation

$$s = \frac{gt^2}{2},$$

using for the purpose what may be regarded as an algebraical artifice—in reality, disguised *integration.*

Before showing how this process illustrates integration, let us examine Newton's geometrical way of dealing with a problem such as the above. *Note how cumbersome both processes are.*

Let the time t be represented by the straight line AB, Fig. 1, and the velocity acquired at the end of time t (from rest), by the straight line BC at right angles to AB. Now suppose AB divided into a number of small equal parts, say into n parts, each equal to MN; and from all such points as M, N, set up straight lines MP, NQ at right angles to AB, and each taken to represent the velocity at the end of the times represented by AM, AN, &c., respectively. Since the velocity is proportional to the time, it is obvious that all such points as P and Q will lie on the straight line AC (for, otherwise, we should not have PM : QN : BC, &c. :: AM : AN : AB). Now, if we suppose the falling body to move during any small portion of time represented by MN, with the velocity at the beginning of that time, represented by **PM**, **the space traversed by the** body in that interval would **be represented by the** rectangle PN ; whereas, **if the** falling body moves during this **interval with the** velocity represented **by QN**, acquired **at the end of** it, **the** space traversed **will be represented by the** rectangle **mN**. The area, then,

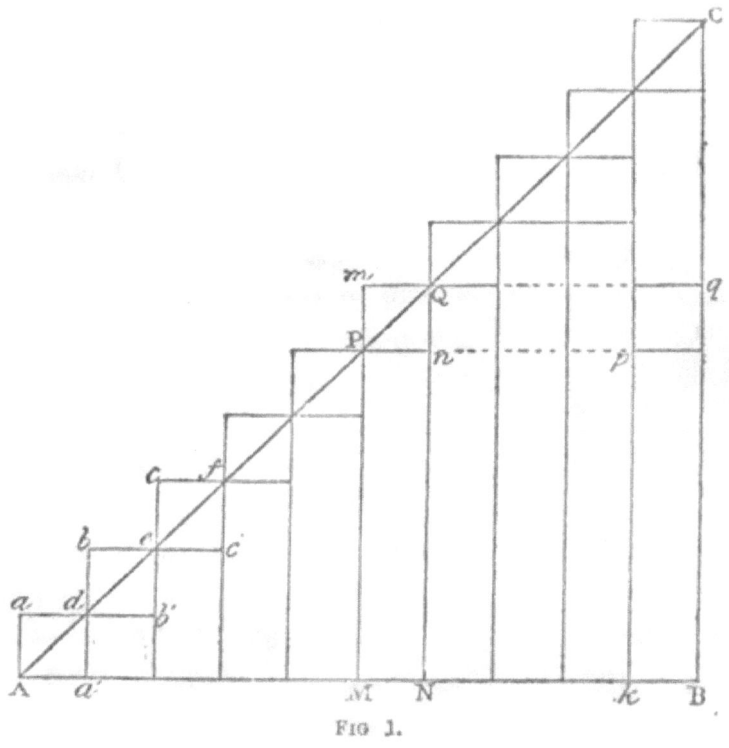

FIG 1.

representing the space actually traversed, lies some- **where** between the two rectangles PN and mN. Thus, the **total** space described in **time** t is repre- sented by an area less than the area between AB, **BC,** and the outer zigzag A*adbecf* &c., and greater than the area between AB, **BC,** and the inner zigzag

$a'db'ec'f$, &c. These areas differ from each other by the sum of the small parallelograms aa', bb', cc', &c. Now although, when n is made very great, and therefore each rectangle like mn very small, the number of such small rectangles is very great, this by no means prevents their sum becoming very small. For sliding the rectangle mn along, parallel to the base AB, to the position pq, and doing the like for all the small rectangles, we have them finally covering the rectangle Ck; and the area of this rectangle becomes as small as we please, when (n being taken as large as we please) kB becomes as small as we please. Therefore the area of the triangle ABC, which lies between the two just named, may be made to differ from either by an area less than any that can be assigned; and this is the same as saying that this area correctly represents the space fallen through from rest under the action of gravity. Now $AB = t$, and $BC = gt$. Hence

$$\text{area } ABC = \frac{gt^2}{2}; \quad \text{and } s = \frac{gt^2}{2}.$$

[The reader must not fall into the mistake of supposing that we are here equating a distance to a triangle. AB represents a period of time, and BC a velocity—in this way only, that the number of units of length in AB are supposed to correspond to the number of units of time in t, &c. Just as we get the right *number* for the square feet in a rectangle by multiplying the *numbers* representing the lengths of the sides, though feet cannot be multiplied by feet to give square feet, so here we get a correct *numerical* result, by using the lengths of lines to represent numbers.]

Now, in each of the above processes, we have employed an artifice, algebraical in one case, geometrical in another, to obtain a result such as the integral calculus obtains in a systematic manner.

We know in this case that the velocity at the end of any time t is gt, or, in other words, that the rate at which the space traversed is increasing, after time t has elapsed from rest, is gt. And we showed in Lesson I. that the differential coefficient of $\frac{gt^2}{2}$ with respect to t is gt, explaining this to mean that the rate of increase of the expression $\frac{gt^2}{2}$ with the variation of t is represented by gt.

Supposing, then, that, in dealing with the fall of a body under gravity, we know the velocity at time t from rest—or the rate of increase of s, the space traversed at this time—to be gt, and also know that gt is the differential coefficient of $\frac{gt^2}{2}$ with respect to t—we can at once write

$$s = \frac{gt^2}{2} + \text{some constant.}$$

(It has not, indeed, been yet shown that two quantities can only have the same differential coefficient when they are either equal or differ by a constant quantity; but for the **present this** is assumed, as we **are now only illustrating the** nature and **use of** differential coefficients, &c.) **And** since when $t = 0$, $s = 0$, the constant must be zero. So that we have, simply,

$$s = \frac{gt^2}{2}.$$

In other words, from our knowledge that $\frac{gt^2}{2}$ is the quantity having gt for its differential coefficient with respect to t, we are at once able to say **that a** falling **body** whose velocity at time t is gt, **will in** time t from rest traverse the space $\frac{gt^2}{2}$. The notation employed for stating this is as follows:—Note that what we have to determine is the **sum of the** spaces described in the infinitely small intervals of time into which the **whole time** t **is** supposed divided; in other words, the **sum** of a number of **small** spaces, each represented by $gt.\Delta t$ where Δt is the increment of the time. **This sum,** which we should represent by $\Sigma gt.\Delta t$, **were the** number **of** spaces not infinite, **is in the** integral calculus represented by $\int gt.dt$ when the number is **infinitely** great and Δt infinitely **small,** and we write

$$\int gt.dt = \frac{gt^2}{2} + \text{a constant.}$$

How **we** find the **sum** corresponding to particular

limiting values of the variable will be shown further on.

Of course, we have here selected a case where we knew beforehand that quantity of which the simple expression we were dealing with is the differential coefficient. In other cases, we might have more or less trouble to determine this; but a great number of differential coefficients are known, and in every such case we can at once write down the expressions of which they are the differential coefficients—or, in other words, we can at once solve our problem. For other cases there are methods by which either an exact or approximate solution can be readily worked out.

To sum up the elementary points thus far illustrated:—

I. *When there is a quantity whose value depends on some variable, the* DIFFERENTIAL COEFFICIENT *of the quantity with respect to that variable represents the rate at which the quantity varies as the variable changes in value.*

II. *When we know the rate at which a quantity depending on some variable changes with change of the variable—in other words, when we know the differential coefficient of the quantity with respect to that variable—we can determine the quantity itself (called the* INTEGRAL), *if only we know what quantity it is which has that differential coefficient.*

When we have indicated how the differential coefficients of a number of expressions can be determined, the importance of these points will be recognised.

LESSON III.

ILLUSTRATIONS OF THE USE OF THE CALCULUS.

THE plan we adopted in Lesson I. to obtain the differential coefficient of the expression $\frac{1}{2} gt^2$ with respect to the variable t, will give us the differential coefficient of many other variable expressions.

It may be well to try one other case, giving also an illustration of the value of such processes, before proceeding to obtain the differential coefficients of various familiar functions.

Suppose, for instance, that

$$x = ay - y^2 \quad \cdots \quad \cdots \quad \cdots \quad \text{(i.)}$$

Increase x by Δx, and y by Δy; then

$$x + \Delta x = a(y + \Delta y) - [y^2 + 2y\Delta y + (\Delta y)^2] \cdots \text{(ii.)}$$

so that, subtracting (i.) from (ii.),

$$\Delta x = a\Delta y - 2y\Delta y - (\Delta y)^2$$

$$\text{and } \frac{\Delta x}{\Delta y} = a - 2y - \Delta y.$$

Now make Δx and Δy infinitely small, calling them dx and dy. Then we get

$$\frac{dx}{dy} = a - 2y - dy = a - 2y.$$

c

This process would be very cumbrous if applied to complex expressions. Therefore, the first matter considered in treatises on the differential calculus, is the determination of rules by which a differential coefficient may be readily obtained. In the next lesson on the subject I shall give some of these rules, without dwelling at any great length on the reasoning by which they are established. Much of this reasoning, indeed, would be beyond those for whose special service these lessons are written. The advantage derived from the practical application of the differential calculus to problems not easily solved in other ways, will encourage the student to discuss after a while the reasoning by which the rules of the calculus have been established. The great difficulty has hitherto been that this reasoning, coming before the student has learned the power of the calculus, has, by its length and complexity, prevented many from pursuing the study of the subject.

But even at this stage, it will be well to illustrate the application of the differential calculus.

Suppose we had this problem given :—

The length of the line AB (Fig. 2) *is* a; *where must a point P be taken in order that the rectangle under AP, PB may be as great as possible?*

A *y* P B

FIG. 2.

Since AP is *y*, PB is $(a - y)$, and the rectangle under AP, PB (which call *x*) is $y (a - y)$; that is

$$x = ay - y^2.$$

We want x to be as great as possible. Now the differential coefficient of x with respect to y, is the rate at which x increases with increase of y (from 0 to a); and so long as x is increasing, x is not as great as possible. We must find then when x ceases to increase, or when its rate of increase (or its differential coefficient) is reduced to nought. Now we have seen that when

$$x = ay - y^2,$$
$$\frac{dx}{dy} = a - 2y.$$

Putting this equal to nought, we have the equation

$$a - 2y = 0,$$
$$\text{or } y = \frac{a}{2}.$$

So that P must bisect AB, in order that the rectangle under AP, PB may be a maximum.

Here is another problem :—

AC (Fig. 3) *is a cylinder constructed to fulfil the condition that its height AB added to AO, the radius of a circular face, is equal to a fixed length a. Required the height* of the cylinder in order *that its curved surface may be as great as possible.*

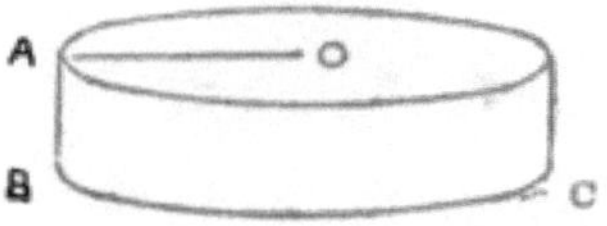

FIG. 3.

Put AB = y; so that AO = $a - y$.

Then the curved surface, which we call x, is represented by the rectangle under the height and the circumference of a circular face. That is (representing the ratio of the circumference to the diameter as usual by π),

$$x = 2\pi(a - y)y = 2\pi(ay - y^2).$$

Here, as before, we must have the rate of increase of x with increase of y (or the differential coefficient of x) *nought*. But if we went through the process for determining the differential coefficient as above, we should readily get

$$\frac{dx}{dy} = 2\pi(a - 2y),$$

and the equation

$$2\pi(a - 2y) = 0$$

gives

$$y = \frac{a}{2},$$

or the height of the cylinder must be equal to the radius of its base.

LESSON IV.

DIFFERENTIATING SIMPLE FUNCTIONS.

WE are now to consider the differential coefficients of certain familiar expressions, and to lay down rules by which the differential coefficient of any expression can be readily determined.

In the first place, let me note that, for convenience, the quantity whose differential coefficient is to be determined is commonly called either y or u; and the quantity whose variation causes the former to change is commonly expressed by x. I select y for the former and retain x for the latter purpose. Let it be remembered that there is no real necessity for any fixed practice in this matter. In the last lesson, for example, I used in one case s and t instead of y and x, while in the other example I interchanged x and y.

Let me repeat that the differential coefficient of one quantity y with respect to another x, is an expression indicating the rate at which the former *increases* as we increase the latter. I advisedly use the word *increase* as respects y, even though increase of x may cause decrease of y. For in such a case the differential coefficient will come out *negative*, and a negative increase is the true algebraical equivalent of decrease.

And now for the differential coefficients of the simple functions.

If $y = a$, or is constant, its differential coefficient with respect to x is of course 0.

Let $y = x^n$, where n is a positive whole number. In this case we will go through the process for finding the differential coefficient. We increase x by Δx, and assume that y is thus increased by Δy.[1] Then

$$y + \Delta y = (x + \Delta x)^n$$
$$= x^n + nx^{n-1}\Delta x$$
$$+ \begin{cases} \text{a finite number of terms in-} \\ \text{volving } (\Delta x)^2, (\Delta x)^3, \&c. \end{cases}$$

and $y = x^n$.

Therefore subtracting

$$\Delta y = nx^{n-1}\Delta x$$
$$+ \begin{cases} \text{terms involving higher powers of } \Delta x \\ \text{than the first.} \end{cases}$$

[1] It is most important to remember that Δx is a single quantity, not Δ multiplied by x, but the increment of x. In the old notation of fluxions, a simple expression was used. But in advanced applications of the differential calculus, the notation of fluxions fails totally, and the dx's and dy's alone serve the mathematician's purpose. Dots represented differentiation in the old system of fluxional notation; a circumstance which led Babbage to make the quaint jest respecting the labours of Peacock, John Herschel, and others, at Cambridge, that they substituted d-ism for the dotage of fluxions.

Hence,

$$\frac{\Delta y}{\Delta x} = nx^{n-1} + \text{terms involving } \Delta x \text{ and its powers.}$$

Now, suppose Δx, and therefore Δy, to become indefinitely minute, calling them respectively dx and dy, and we have

$$\frac{dy}{dx} = nx^{n-1} + \begin{cases} \text{a finite number of inde-} \\ \text{finitely minute quantities} \end{cases}$$
$$= nx^{n-1}.$$

The extension of this proof to the cases where n is fractional or negative, or both, would not suit these lessons. Let it suffice that for all values of n

$$\text{if } y = x^n$$
$$\frac{dy}{dx} = nx^{n-1}.$$

But let us remove this result from the region of algebraical expressions for a moment, in order that its significance, and the significance of sequent results, may be fully recognised. Take x to be 10, and n to be 4, then

$$y = 10^4 = 10000.$$

Try now the effect of adding to x some small quantity, say 1-100th, or ·01. Then instead of 10^4, y becomes $(10\cdot01)^4$, and if we calculate the value of this, we find it to be

$$10040\cdot06004001.$$

The effective part of the increment of y is the 40, and the proportion it bears to the increment of x (or 1-100th) is 4000. This is 4 times the cube of 10, or nx^{n-1}. And so in any case the reader may care to try : whenever $y = x^n$, a minute increase in the value of x gives to y an increase nx^{n-1} times as great.

The general result enables us to at once express the differential coefficient of all such quantities as

$$\sqrt{x}, \quad \sqrt[3]{x}, \quad \frac{1}{x^2},$$

and so on. It is only necessary to write these (or conceive them written), in the forms $x^{\frac{1}{2}}$, $x^{\frac{1}{3}}$, x^{-2}, to see that the respective differential coefficients are

$$\tfrac{1}{2} x^{-\frac{1}{2}}, \quad \tfrac{1}{3}x^{-\frac{2}{3}}, \text{ and } - 2x^{-3},$$

which we may write respectively

$$\frac{1}{2\sqrt{x}}, \quad \frac{1}{3\sqrt[3]{x^2}}, \text{ and } - \frac{2}{x^3}.$$

Any one who has become at all practised in applying the differential calculus, would of course write down these results at once. It is plain, too, from the mode of proof that if $y = ax^n$, where a is constant,

$$\frac{dy}{dx} = anx^{n-1}.$$

The next simple function I shall take is the sine of an angle. And having in view the importance of the reader's obtaining clear views of the nature of a differential coefficient, I shall in this case employ a geometrical way of finding such a coefficient.

Let the angle x be represented by AOB, Fig. 4; then, using the arc measure and making the radius unity, we have

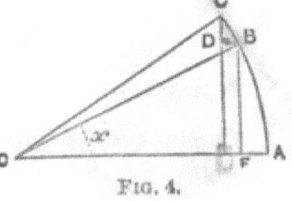

FIG. 4.

$$x = \text{arc } AB,$$

and $\sin x = BF$, where BF is perpendicular to OA,

$$= y \text{ suppose.}$$

Now let angle AOB receive the small increment BOC, and call the arc BC, Δx; then, completing the figure, the corresponding increment of the sine is CD. Hence

$$\frac{\Delta y}{\Delta x} = \frac{CD}{CB}.$$

Now it is clear that as C is brought nearer and nearer to B, the figure BCD approaches more and more nearly to the figure of a triangle similar to BOF; and therefore, the ratio $\frac{CD}{CB}$ approaches more and more nearly to the ratio $\frac{OF}{OB}$. Hence when C so moving is *just coming* upon B (in which state of things let BC be called dx, and CD be called dy) we have

$$\frac{dy}{dx} = \frac{OF}{OB} = \cos x.^{[1]}$$

---

[1] The reader should very carefully note that this is not an approximate result, but exact. In all these cases, where limits

We have then, if

$$y = \sin x,$$
$$\frac{dy}{dx} = \cos x.$$

Let **us** study this result a little.

Remembering that the differential coefficient of a quantity expresses the rate at which the quantity is

are dealt with, we **are compelled** to consider approximate *cases* in order to learn the nature of the final state of things; but **our** *result* refers to *that* state **of** things, and not **to any intermediate** state, *however near.* The reader has missed the essential point of the method of limits if he fails to **see this.** We have **not** to deal with approximate *results* at all in thus applying the method. Perhaps the beginner may recognise this truth more clearly if I apply the method to solve a well-known problem. Let it be required to determine **the angle** ABT, in**cluded between a** radius AB of the circle BCF (Fig. 5), and **the** tangent BT at B. Take C a point near B, **and draw** the secant CBD. Then conceive that C approaches B, carrying **the secant** along with it. Obviously when C has thus moved up to B, **the** secant will occupy the position of the tangent BT. Now in any antecedent position, as C in the figure, we **have** the triangle ABC isosceles; and the equal angles ABC, **ACB to**gether, differ from two right angles by the angle A. Hence ABC falls short of a right angle by half the angle A; so that **ABD (which** together with ABC makes up two right angles) exceeds a right **angle by** half the angle A. Now when C moves up to B, the angle A diminishes, and ultimately vanishes. **Hence** the difference between ABD **and a** right angle ultimately vanishes; so that when the secant CBD **has** become the tangent BT, the angle ABT is a right angle. We know this to be not approximately, but exactly, true; but the reader must not be satisfied until he sees that the line of reasoning given here *proves* it to be so.

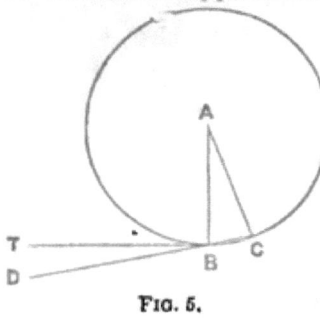

FIG. 5.

increasing, we see that the above result implies that as we increase the angle the sine increases, until x is a right angle or $\frac{\pi}{2}$. But after x has passed this value, $\cos x$ is negative. This implies that the sine thenceforth diminishes; and we know as a matter of fact that the sine does diminish as the angle passes the right angle.

Notice, also, how the differential coefficient implies the rate of change. We know that $\cos x$ is unity, or has its greatest value, when $x = 0$. As x changes from 0, then, the sine changes fastest. Again: $\cos x$ is nought when x is a right angle, and very small when x is nearly a right angle. Hence the sine changes very slowly as the angle is passing the right angle. All this, of course, is very obvious without any reference to the differential calculus. But it serves well to illustrate the application of the calculus to more difficult inquiries.

Obviously, if

$$y = a \sin x,$$
$$\frac{dy}{dx} = a \cos x,$$

In the next Lesson a similar method will be applied to others of the trigonometrical ratios.

LESSON V.

DIFFERENTIATING SIMPLE FUNCTIONS (*continued*).

IT may be well to apply the method already used to determine the differential coefficient of sin x, to the other simple trigonometrical functions; for not only does the method indicate well what a differential coefficient is, but as all these functions are dealt with in the same way, the memory is aided to retain all their differential coefficients.

As before, we use the circular measure for angles, and regard radius as unity. The construction of the diagram (Fig. 6, p. 30) is obvious.

$$\text{Put arc } AB = x, \; Bb = \Delta x.$$

Then we have seen that if

$$y = \sin x; \; \frac{dy}{dx} = \cos x.$$

Put now

$$y = \cos x = Om,$$

radius being unity. Then

$$\Delta y = \cos (x + \Delta x) - \cos x = Ok - Om = - km$$

$$\therefore \frac{\Delta y}{\Delta x} = - \frac{km}{Bb} = - \frac{l B}{B b};$$

and when Δx and Δy are both indefinitely small, we have

$$\frac{l\mathrm{B}}{\mathrm{B}b} = \frac{\mathrm{B}m}{\mathrm{OB}} = \sin x$$

$$\therefore \text{ when } y = \cos x;\ \frac{dy}{dx} = -\sin x.$$

Put next

$$y = \tan x = \mathrm{AT}.$$

Describe arc $\mathrm{T}n$ about O as centre. Then

$$\Delta y = \tan (x + \Delta x) - \tan x = t\mathrm{A} - \mathrm{TA} = \mathrm{T}t.$$

$$\therefore \frac{\Delta y}{\Delta x} = \frac{\mathrm{T}t}{\mathrm{B}b} = \frac{\mathrm{T}t}{\mathrm{T}n} \cdot \frac{\mathrm{T}n}{\mathrm{B}b} = \frac{\mathrm{T}t}{\mathrm{T}n} \cdot \frac{\mathrm{TO}}{\mathrm{BO}};$$

and when Δx and Δy are both indefinitely small, we have

$$\frac{\mathrm{T}t}{\mathrm{T}n} = \frac{\mathrm{OB}}{\mathrm{O}m} = \sec x;$$

and

$$\frac{\mathrm{TO}}{\mathrm{BO}} = \frac{\mathrm{TO}}{\mathrm{OA}} = \sec x.$$

So that when

$$y = \tan x,\ \frac{dy}{dx} = \sec^2 x = \frac{1}{\cos^2 x}.$$

When $y = \cot x$, we have a precisely similar construction; but we may here conveniently use the same construction which has given us $\tan x$ to give us $\cot x$. For this purpose we set OC at right angles to OA and call the arc $\mathrm{C}b$, x; and $b\mathrm{B}$, Δx.

Then we get At for cot x and $\mathbf{A}T$ for cot $(x + \Delta x)$. So that we have the same difference Tt, only in this

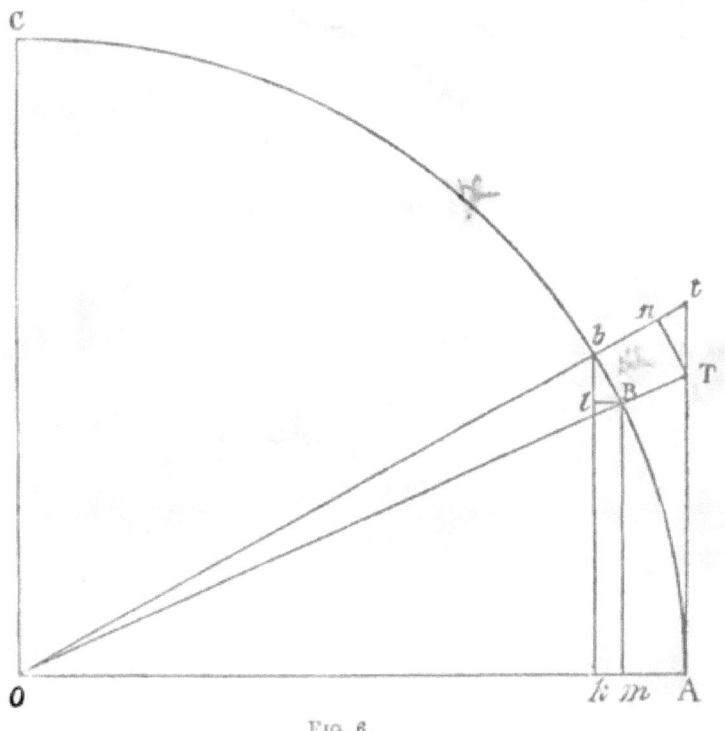

FIG. 6.

case it **is a** diminution instead of an increase. We have also

$$\frac{TO}{BO} = \frac{TO}{OA} = \sec BA = \operatorname{cosec} CB = \operatorname{cosec} x$$

(when Bb vanishes). Hence when

$$y = \cot x; \quad \frac{dy}{dx} = -\operatorname{cosec}^2 x = -\frac{1}{\sin^2 x}.$$

Next take

$$y = \sec x = OT.$$

Then

$$\Delta y = \sec(x + \Delta x) - \sec x = Ot - OT = nt;$$

$$\therefore \frac{\Delta y}{\Delta x} = \frac{nt}{Bb} = \frac{nt}{Tn} \cdot \frac{Tn}{Bb};$$

and when Δx and Δy are both indefinitely small, we have

$$\frac{nt}{Tn} = \frac{AT}{OA} = \tan x;$$

while $\dfrac{nT}{Bb}$ as before $= \sec x.$

So that, when

$$y = \sec x; \quad \frac{dy}{dx} = \tan x \cdot \sec x = \frac{\sin x}{\cos^2 x}$$

And similarly, calling COb, x, as in dealing with the cotangent, we find when

$$y = \operatorname{cosec} x; \quad \frac{dy}{dx} = -\cot . x \operatorname{cosec} x = -\frac{\cos x}{\sin^2 x}.$$

The student should have the differential co-efficients of the six simple trigonometrical functions at his fingers' ends, as they are constantly wanted. The six functions are here collected into the three which have positive differential coefficients (for arcs less than a quadrant), the sine, tangent, and secant; and those which have negative differential coefficients, the cosine, the cotangent, and cosecant.

$$\text{If } y = \sin x; \quad \frac{dy}{dx} = \cos x$$

$$y = \tan x; \quad \frac{dy}{dx} = \frac{1}{\cos^2 x}$$

$$y = \sec x; \quad \frac{dy}{dx} = \frac{\sin x}{\cos^2 x}$$

$$y = \cos x; \quad \frac{dy}{dx} = -\sin x$$

$$y = \cot x; \quad \frac{dy}{dx} = -\frac{1}{\sin^2 x}$$

$$y = \operatorname{cosec} x; \quad \frac{dy}{dx} = -\frac{\cos x}{\sin^2 x}$$

Let us next try the inverse trigonometrical functions, and see whether they admit of similar treatment.

Take $y = \sin^{-1} x$. Then in Fig. 6 we may represent y by the arc BA, whose sin is Bm, so that Bm represents x.

Thus $y = $ BA
$x = $ Bm
Put $bl = \Delta x$; so that $(x + \Delta x) = bk$.
Then $\Delta y = \sin^{-1}(x + \Delta x) - \sin^{-1} \Delta x$
$= \text{arc } Ab - \text{arc } AB$
$= Bb$
$\therefore \frac{\Delta y}{\Delta x} = \frac{Bb}{bl}$.

Now when Δy and Δx are both indefinitely small

$$\frac{Bb}{bl} = \frac{BO}{Om} = \sec y.$$

Hence, when

$$y = \sin^{-1}x \; ; \quad \frac{dy}{dx} = \sec y = \frac{1}{\sqrt{1 - \sin^2 y}} = \frac{1}{\sqrt{1 - x^2}}.$$

Applying a similar method to the other simple inverse fractions, we find

If $y = \cos^{-1}x$; $\quad \dfrac{dy}{dx} = -\operatorname{cosec} y = \dfrac{-1}{\sqrt{1 - x^2}}$

If $y = \tan^{-1}x$; $\quad \dfrac{dy}{dx} = \cos^2 y \qquad = \dfrac{1}{1 + x^2}$,

If $y = \cot^{-1}x$; $\quad \dfrac{dy}{dx} = -\sin^2 y \qquad = \dfrac{-1}{1 + x^2}$

If $y = \sec^{-1}x$; $\quad \dfrac{dy}{dx} = \dfrac{\cos^2 y}{\sin y} \qquad = \dfrac{1}{x\sqrt{x^2 - 1}}$

If $y = \operatorname{cosec}^{-1}x$; $\dfrac{dy}{dx} = -\dfrac{\sin^2 y}{\cos y} \qquad = \dfrac{-1}{x\sqrt{x^2 - 1}}$

The student will find no trouble whatever in obtaining any of these results. He will find in every case, on making the geometrical construction (or examining that already made, for Fig. 6 illustrates all the cases) that the value of $\frac{\Delta y}{\Delta x}$ in the case of an inverse function is the reciprocal of the value of $\frac{\Delta y}{\Delta x}$ in the case of the corresponding direct function. For instance, in dealing with $y = \sin^{-1}x$,

D

we found $\dfrac{\Delta y}{\Delta x}$ to be $\dfrac{Bb}{bl}$, whereas in dealing with $y = \sin^{-1}x$, we had found

$$\frac{\Delta y}{\Delta x} = \frac{bl}{Bb}.$$

This was to be expected, when we consider that to say $y = \sin^{-1}x$ is the same as to say $x = \sin y$; so that x and y are simply interchanged in passing from the consideration of a direct function to the consideration of the corresponding inverse function. Nevertheless, it would not be sound at this stage of our inquiry to determine $\dfrac{dy}{dx}$ from this consideration only. Under certain limitations, which we need not consider here, it may be assumed that $\dfrac{dy}{dx}$ is the reciprocal of $\dfrac{dx}{dy}$. But at present we regard $\dfrac{dy}{dx}$ as a single expression. It is derived from $\dfrac{\Delta y}{\Delta x}$ by supposing Δy and Δx to diminish indefinitely. Now, when Δy has any definite value, and therefore Δx a definite value, it is of course true that $\dfrac{\Delta y}{\Delta x}$ is the reciprocal of $\dfrac{\Delta x}{\Delta y}$; but we must not assume that *of necessity* the value to which $\dfrac{\Delta x}{\Delta y}$ tends with the indefinite diminution of Δy and Δx is the reciprocal of the value to which $\dfrac{\Delta y}{\Delta x}$ tends under the same conditions. This would be assuming that we can treat dx and dy as themselves definite quantities, whereas they are in reality indefinite, though they bear to each other a definite relation. It would matter very little so far as the dx and dy of the simple $\frac{dy}{dx}$ are concerned, that we should treat these as separable quantities; but as we advance with the calculus we find occasion to differentiate differential coefficients, and we are led to the use of such forms as

$$\frac{d^2y}{dx^2}, \frac{d^3y}{dx^3}, \&c.;$$

and it would be altogether inadmissible to regard the dx^2 and the dx^3 of these expressions as if they were the square and cube of the dx in the expression $\frac{dy}{dx}$.

Of course when, after starting from, say, the statement

$$y = \sec^{-1}x,$$

we find

$$\frac{dy}{dx} = \frac{\cos^2 y}{\sin y},$$

it is easy to express this result in terms of x; for we have

$$x = \sec y.$$

So that

$$\cos y = \frac{1}{x}, \text{ and } \sin y = \sqrt{1 - \frac{1}{x^2}}.$$

I might here give some examples illustrating the application of the differential calculus—with the coefficients already determined—to various problems of interest. But it will be well **first to get** over so **much elementary** ground **as** is involved **in the** determination of rules for differentiating all expressions **whatever.** For **then we can** take a **much more** varied range of examples than we **could by limiting** ourselves to **the application of** what we have **already** learned. It is seldom **in** physical questions that **we** are limited **to simple** trigonometrical functions, **and** we could scarcely advance half-a-dozen steps without feeling the necessity of **rules for** finding the differential coefficients of complex functions and functions of functions. Indeed we should have found the use **of such rules in** simplifying **what we have** already **done, only that it seemed well to have a few** examples **of the process of** obtaining **a differential** coefficient **directly. Otherwise when** we **had to** consider, say, $y = \sec x$, **we might** have regarded y **as a** function of $\cos x$, **and proceeded from**

$$y = \frac{1}{\cos x}$$

to write down the differential coefficient. Again we **might** have written, for $y = \tan x$

$$y = \sin x \cdot \sec x,$$

and at once written down $\dfrac{dy}{dx}$, if we had the rules,

which I shall proceed to examine and establish (as
far as is necessary in such elementary lessons as these)
in Lesson VI. Then we can proceed to discuss a
few problems which will not only show the great
value of the calculus, but also illustrate the real
meaning of what we have thus far done.

I may, however, here pause to note that the
reader must not allow himself to be mystified by the
use of such an expression as 'differential coefficient,'
a term which might seem expressly devised to deter
the young mathematician from the study of the
calculus, as implying that it cannot possibly be of
any practical use—at any rate, in simple problems.
For what idea of utility does the expression 'differential coefficient' convey? and why should an expression be employed really belonging to a matter
with which elementary applications of the calculus are
in no way concerned?—*viz.*, the expansion of sundry
functions in the form of series, of which what we are
calling the differential coefficient is one of the coefficients. What the young student has to bear in
mind is that what (to avoid the invention of new
terms) we call the differential coefficient, is in reality
a quantity indicating the rate at which whatever
function—simple or complex—we want to deal with,
changes with the change of the variable it involves.
When we consider how many problems depend on
such changes and cannot possibly be dealt with unless
we can determine their effects and limits, the import-

ance of a calculus devised for this purpose will **be at** once obvious. We shall very soon be able to show this, for we shall very soon have completed our inquiry into methods **by which the** rate of increase of **any** quantity whatever, **as** its variable increases, **can be** determined.

LESSON VI.

DIFFERENTIATING COMPOSITE FUNCTIONS.

WE have now to establish rules for dealing with composite functions, and functions of functions.

First let us take composite functions—viz. (i.) the sums and differences of functions; (ii.) the products of functions; (iii.) functions divided by functions.

I. Let $u = v + w - y + z$, &c., where v, w, y, z, &c., are all functions of x; and when x is altered into $(x + \Delta x)$, let u be altered into $(u + \Delta u)$, v into $(v + \Delta v)$, w into $(w + \Delta w)$, &c. Then

$$u + \Delta u = (v + \Delta v) + (w + \Delta w) - (y + \Delta y) \\ + (z + \Delta z) + \text{&c.}$$

Hence, subtracting the former equation from the latter,

$$\Delta u = \Delta v + \Delta w - \Delta y + \Delta z + \text{&c.,}$$

and dividing both sides by Δx, we have

$$\frac{\Delta u}{\Delta x} = \frac{\Delta v}{\Delta x} + \frac{\Delta w}{\Delta x} - \frac{\Delta y}{\Delta x} + \frac{\Delta z}{\Delta x} + \text{&c.}$$

Now, suppose Δx to become indefinitely small, so that

$$\frac{\Delta u}{\Delta x}, \frac{\Delta v}{\Delta x}, \frac{\Delta w}{\Delta x}, \frac{\Delta y}{\Delta x}, \frac{\Delta z}{\Delta x}, \text{&c.,}$$

become the differential coefficients of u, v, w, y, z, &c., with respect to x. Then we have

$$\frac{du}{dx} = \frac{dv}{dx} + \frac{dw}{dx} - \frac{dy}{dx} + \frac{dz}{dx} + \&c. \qquad (A)$$

II. Let $u = y\,z$; y, z, as before, being functions of x, and the same changes taking place in u, y, z, when x is changed into $x + \Delta x$. Then,

$$u + \Delta u = (y + \Delta y)(z + \Delta z)$$
$$= yz + z\Delta y + y\Delta z + \Delta y\Delta z,$$

and subtracting the former from the latter

$$\Delta u = z\Delta y + y\Delta z + \Delta y\Delta z$$

and

$$\frac{\Delta u}{\Delta x} = z\frac{\Delta y}{\Delta x} + y\frac{\Delta z}{\Delta x} + \frac{\Delta y\Delta z}{\Delta x}.$$

Now when Δx is made indefinitely small, this becomes

$$\frac{du}{dx} = z\frac{dy}{dx} + y\frac{dz}{dx} + \frac{dy}{dx}\text{(an indefinitely small quantity)}$$

or

$$\frac{du}{dx} = z\frac{dy}{dx} + y\frac{dz}{dx}.$$

And in like manner it may be shown that if

$$u = vyz\ldots$$

$$\frac{du}{dx} = yz\ldots\frac{dv}{dx} + vz\ldots\frac{dy}{dx} + vy\ldots\frac{dz}{dx} + \&c. \qquad (B)$$

III. Let

$$u = \frac{y}{z},$$

y and z being functions of x. Then

$$u + \Delta u = \frac{y + \Delta y}{z + \Delta z} = \frac{y}{z}\left(1 + \frac{\Delta y}{y}\right)\left(1 + \frac{\Delta z}{z}\right)^{-1}$$

$$= \frac{y}{z}\left(1 + \frac{\Delta y}{y}\right)\left(1 - \frac{\Delta z}{z}\right.$$

$$\left. + \text{ terms involving } (\Delta z)^2, \&c.\right)$$

$$= \frac{y}{z} + \frac{\Delta y}{z} - \frac{y \cdot \Delta z}{z^2}$$

$$+ (\text{terms involving } \Delta y . \Delta z, \Delta z^2, \&c.)$$

∴ Subtracting

$$\Delta u = \frac{\Delta y}{z} - \frac{y \cdot \Delta z}{z^2} + (\text{terms involving } \Delta z^2, \&c. \text{ And}$$

$$\frac{\Delta u}{\Delta x} = \frac{1}{z}\frac{\Delta y}{\Delta x} - \frac{y}{z^2} \cdot \frac{\Delta z}{\Delta x} + (\text{terms involving } \Delta z^2, \&c.)$$

so that proceeding to the limit,

$$\frac{du}{dx} = \frac{1}{z}\frac{dy}{dx} - \frac{y}{z^2}\frac{dz}{dx} \tag{C}$$

which may be written in the easily remembered form

$$\frac{du}{dx} = \frac{1}{z^2}\left(z\frac{dy}{dx} - y\frac{dz}{dx}\right). \tag{C}$$

Take next a function of a function. Suppose, for instance, that $u = \phi(y)$, where y is a function of x.

Let y change to $y + \Delta y$ when Δy is some small but finite increment, and with this change let u become $u + \Delta u$, and x become $x + \Delta x$. Then we have

$$u + \Delta u = \phi(y + \Delta y)$$
$$\Delta u = \phi(y + \Delta y) - \phi(y)$$

and

$$\frac{\Delta u}{\Delta x} = \frac{\phi(y + \Delta y) - \phi(y)}{\Delta x}$$

$$= \frac{\phi(y + \Delta y) - \phi(y)}{\Delta y} \cdot \frac{\Delta y}{\Delta x}.$$

Now let Δy become indefinitely small, Δu and Δx becoming also indefinitely small. Then

$$\frac{\phi(y + \Delta y) - \phi(y)}{\Delta y} \text{ becomes } \frac{du}{dy},$$

in accordance with our definition of a differential coefficient, and the above equation becomes

$$\frac{du}{dx} = \frac{du}{dy} \cdot \frac{dy}{dx}. \tag{D}$$

If we note that relation (C) may be written thus,

$$\frac{du}{dx} = \frac{1}{z} \cdot \frac{dy}{dx} + y\frac{d(\frac{1}{z})}{dx}$$

(a relation not apparent until **D** had been established) we see that relations A, B, and C may be combined into the first of the following rules, while D gives the second : —

Rule **I.**—*To determine the differential coefficient* of a composite function *of a variable, with respect to this* variable, differentiate each component *function* with respect to the *variable* as *if the rest were constant,* and add the *results.*

Rule II.—*To* **determine** *the differential coefficient of a function* **of a** *function of a variable, with respect to this variable, differentiate with respect* to *the* **last-**mentioned *function, and multiply the result* by *the differential coefficient of this function with respect to the* **variable.**

It is hardly necessary to note that *the differential coefficient of a constant is zero,* for this is only another way of saying that a constant does not vary. It is also clear that *if the differential coefficient of a quantity is zero, the quantity must be constant,* for this is only saying that a quantity which does not vary is constant. It is, moreover, independently obvious, but comes out directly from Rule I., that *if the differential co-efficient of a quantity is known, then the differential coefficient* of the quantity multiplied or **divided** by a constant is the former differential coefficient **multiplied** or divided by the same **constant.**

We had occasion some time back to note that *two* quantities which have the same differential coefficient can only differ by a constant quantity. We can now prove this. For let there be two quantities, y and z, both functions of a variable x, which **have the same** coefficient with respect to x : so that

$$\frac{dy}{dx} = \frac{dz}{dx}.$$

Then, if $y - z = u$, we have, by Rule **1**,

$$\frac{du}{dx} = \frac{dy}{dx} - \frac{dz}{dx} = 0,$$

wherefore u **is a** constant—*i.e.* since $u = y - z$, y can only differ from z by a constant quantity.

In our next we shall **give** some examples of differentiation **by these rules.**

LESSON VII.

ILLUSTRATIONS : MAXIMA AND MINIMA.

In our last lesson we established the general rules for differentiating composite functions, and functions of functions. We now give some examples of the application of these rules. To illustrate the first rule, take the following cases :—

Required the differential coefficient of $a + x - x^2$ with respect to x. The differential coefficient of a is 0, that of x is 1, that of $-x^2$ is $-2x$. Hence, if

$$y = a + x - x^2$$
$$\frac{dy}{dx} = 1 - 2x.$$

Again put

$$y = (a + x - x^2) \sin x.$$

Then the differential coefficient of $(a + x - x^2)$ is $(1 - 2x)$, and the first portion of the required coefficient is therefore

$$(1 - 2x) \sin x.$$

The differential coefficient of $\sin x$ is $\cos x$; and therefore the second part of the required coefficient is

$$(a + x - x^2) \cos x.$$

We add, according to our first rule, and so we get

$$\frac{dy}{dx} = (1 - 2x)\sin x + (a + x - x^2)\cos x.$$

Next, to illustrate the second rule, though we shall presently have to go back to the first :—
Let

$$y = (\sin x)^n.$$

Here y is a function of $\sin x$. So that by the second rule we treat $\sin x$ as if it were the quantity with respect to which y is to be differentiated. We know (see Lesson **IV.**) that if y were equal to x^n, its differential coefficient would be nx^{n-1}. Hence in this case we have for the first factor of our coefficient $n(\sin x)^{n-1}$. But the rule tells us we are to multiply this by the differential coefficient of $\sin x$, that is by $\cos x$. Hence we have finally

$$\frac{dy}{dx} = n(\sin x)^{n-1}\cos x.$$

Take another case.
Let

$$y = (a^2 + x^2)^{\frac{1}{2}}.$$

Here y is a function of $(a^2 + x^2)$. Hence by the second rule we treat $(a^2 + x^2)$ as if it were the quantity with respect to which y is to be differentiated. If y were equal to $x^{\frac{1}{2}}$ we know (see Lesson **IV.**) that its differential coefficient would be

$$\frac{1}{2}x^{-\frac{1}{2}}, \text{ or } \frac{1}{2x^{\frac{1}{2}}}.$$

Hence the **first** factor of the required coefficient is

$$\frac{1}{2(a^2 + x^2)^{\frac{1}{2}}}.$$

We are to multiply this by the differential coefficient of $(a^2 + x^2)$—that is, by $2x$. Therefore we have finally

$$\frac{dy}{dx} = \frac{2x}{2(a^2 + x^2)^{\frac{1}{2}}} = \frac{x}{\sqrt{a^2 + x^2}}.$$

Take **another** case of the second rule.
Let

$$y = \frac{1}{\sin x}.$$

We know that if y were equal to

$$\frac{1}{x} \text{ or } x^{-1}$$

its differential coefficient would be

$$-x^{-2}, \text{ or } -\frac{1}{x^2}.$$

Hence, the first factor of the required coefficient **is**

$$-\frac{1}{(\sin x)^2}.$$

We must multiply this by **the** differential coefficient of $\sin x$, that is **by cos x. Thus we** get finally

$$\frac{dy}{dx} = -\frac{\cos x}{(\sin x)^2} = -\cos x \operatorname{cosec}^2 x.$$

This is one of the results already obtained. But

observe specially that the differential coefficient of
the reciprocal of any quantity may be shown in
precisely the same way to be the reciprocal squared
multiplied by the differential coefficient of the quantity, taken negatively.   For example :—

If

$$y = \frac{1}{a^2 + x^2}$$

$$\frac{dy}{dx} = -\frac{1}{(a^2 + x^2)^2} \times 2x = \frac{-2x}{(a^2 + x^2)^2}.$$

And now finally (so far as the present lesson is concerned) let us take a case in which both of our rules
are applied, but more directly dealt with under sub-
rule C for the case of a function divided by a function.   We will deal with it in both ways, as more
effectively illustrating this part of our subject.

Let

$$y = \frac{\sin x}{\cos x}.$$

By the first rule we get at once the first portion
of the required coefficient.   For, treating cos x as a
constant, we take the differential coefficient of sin x,
that is, cos x, and get the first portion, viz.

$$\frac{\cos x}{\cos x} \text{ or } 1.$$

For the second part we treat sin x as a constant,
and have to multiply it by the differential coefficient

of the other factor $\dfrac{1}{\cos x}$. By what was shown in the preceding case, this is

$$-\frac{1}{\cos^2 x} \times -\sin x, \text{ or } \frac{\sin x}{\cos^2 x}.$$

This multiplied by **sin x gives for** the second portion

$$\frac{\sin^2 x}{\cos^2 x}.$$

Hence the required differential coefficient is

$$1 + \frac{\sin^2 x}{\cos^2 x} = \frac{1}{\cos^2 x}.$$

This would be obtained at once from rule C, which states that where one function is divided by another, the differential coefficient is equal to

$$\frac{\text{numer's dif. coef.}}{\text{denominator}} - \frac{\text{numer.} \times \text{denominator's dif. coef.}}{(\text{denominator})^2};$$

or from the more symmetrical form of the differential coefficient of a fraction—

$$\frac{\text{numer. dif. coef.} \times \text{denom.} - \text{denom. dif. coef.} \times \text{numer.}}{(\text{denominator})^2}.$$

We have now had a good deal of rule-stating and rule-illustrating. In the next lesson some of the rules will be applied to a few problems of maxima and minima. Probably some readers who have begun to grow weary may be induced, when they see the value of the rules, to master them more thoroughly than they have yet done.

E

LESSON VIII.

FURTHER EXAMPLES OF MAXIMA AND MINIMA.

THE following examples may serve conveniently to illustrate the application of even the first principles of the differential calculus to problems which otherwise would present considerable difficulty :—

PROBLEM I.—*A person is in a boat B (Fig. 7) three miles from the nearest point A, of a straight shore line, C D. He wishes to reach E, a point 5 miles from A, as quickly as possible. He can walk 5 miles an hour, but only row 4 miles an hour. Where must he land?*

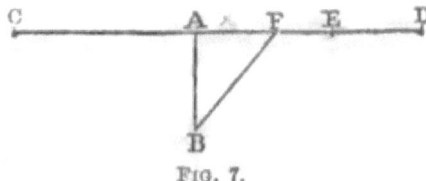

FIG. 7.

Suppose F is the point where he should land, and call AF, *x*. Then BA is perpendicular to CD.

And
$$BF = \sqrt{BA^2 + x^2} = \sqrt{9 + x^2}.$$

Hence, the time taken in traversing BF is

$$\frac{\sqrt{9 + x^2}}{4}.$$

Again,

$$FE = 5 - x,$$

and the time taken in traversing FE is

$$\frac{5 - x}{5}.$$

Thus, if $y =$ total time occupied in reaching E, we have

$$y = \frac{\sqrt{9 + x^2}}{4} + \frac{5 - x}{5}.$$

Now, following the two rules, we get readily,

$$\frac{dy}{dx} = \frac{x}{4\sqrt{9 + x^2}} - \frac{1}{5}.$$

This expresses the rate at which the time increases as F is moved away from A. One can see that when x is very small the value of $\frac{dy}{dx}$ is negative. Since a negative increase is decrease, this shows that our man will get to F more quickly by landing to the right of A (close by) than actually at A. And as long as $\frac{dy}{dx}$ continues negative this shortening continues. But as x increases, we reach at last a value for which $\frac{dy}{dx}$ ceases to be negative and becomes positive, passing through the value *nought*. When x has that value, the shortening has reached

its utmost; so that to obtain the maximum we require, we have only to solve the equation,

$$\frac{x}{4\sqrt{9 + x^2}} - \frac{1}{5} = 0,$$

or, $5x = 4\sqrt{9 + x^2}$,

i.e. $25x^2 = 16\,(9 + x^2)$
$$= 144 + 16x^2.$$

This gives

$$9x^2 = 144$$
$$3x = 12$$
$$x = 4.$$

So that our traveller must land four miles from **A** or
one mile from F.

We see that whether for a maximum or minimum
we must equate $\dfrac{dy}{dx}$ to zero. The question itself will
show whether a maximum or minimum exists for the
deduced value of x.

One more example will close the present lesson.

PROBLEM II.—*A sphere has a radius* r. *What is
the greatest right cone which can be
inscribed in the sphere?*

Let **BD** (Fig. 8), the height of
the cone ABC, be x. Then DC,
the radius of the base, is a mean
proportional between BD and DE.
That is

FIG. 8. $DC = \sqrt{x\,(2r - x)}.$

Hence the area of the base

$$= \pi x (2r - x),$$

and the content of the cone

$$= \pi x (2r - x) \times \frac{x}{3} = \frac{\pi x^2}{3} (2r - x).$$

(I assume a knowledge on the reader's part of the relations between the content and surface of cones, cylinders, spheres, and so on.)

Now, put y for content of cone; that is, put

$$y = \frac{\pi x^2}{3} (2r - x),$$

and find the differential coefficient of y according to the first rule. We can write it down at once, thus,

$$\frac{dy}{dx} = \frac{2\pi x}{3} (2r - x) - \frac{\pi x^2}{3}$$

(the reader will at once see that the two portions of this value are obtained by Rule I., in Lesson VI.)

Now, so long as by increasing x, y increases, we have not a maximum cone. Hence, since the differential coefficient expresses the rate of increase, we must have

$$\frac{dy}{dx} = 0,$$

or

$$\frac{2\pi x}{3} (2r - x) - \frac{\pi x^2}{3} = 0,$$

that is

$$2x (2r - x) = x^2,$$

or

$$4rx = 3x^2 \quad \ldots \ldots \text{(i.)}$$

This gives

$$x = \frac{4r}{3},$$

and therefore **D** must not be where it is shown in Fig. 8, but DE must be equal to twice OD. The reader will notice that (i.) is also satisfied if $x = 0$. We see that when $x = 0$, the volume of the cone is also nought. This is a **minimum not a** maximum **value.** It is clearly **quite as necessary that the differen**tial coefficient **should vanish to give a mini**mum as **to give a maximum. In all cases like the** present, and indeed in nearly **all the** most useful simple applications of the calculus, the conditions of **the** problem itself show us when we have a maximum **or a** minimum. There *are* rules for analytically determining this ; but **I shall** not trouble **the reader** with them. **He** sees **in this case that the content of** the **cone** starts **from 0 when the height is 0, to 0** again when the **height is** $2r$; **hence** at some part **of** the passage from **0 to 0 the** cone **must** have a maximum value; **and the** above **process** shows him (what he could not readily **find by** any other) that the **cone** has its maximum value **when** DE $= 2$ OD.

LESSON IX.

DIFFERENTIATING LOGARITHMIC FUNCTIONS.

Two functions still remain to be dealt with, $\log x$ and a^x, after which the student will be able to differentiate **any functions whatever, simple or complex.**

First, then, let $y = \log_a x$. Increasing x to $x + \triangle x$, whereby y is increased to $y + \triangle y$, and then subtracting, we have

$$\triangle y = \log_a (x + \triangle x) - \log_a x$$

$$= \log_a \left(\frac{x + \triangle x}{x} \right)$$

$$= \log_a \left(1 + \frac{h}{x} \right) \quad \text{writing } h \text{ for } \triangle x, \text{ for convenience.}$$

$$= \frac{1}{\log_e a} \left[\frac{h}{x} - \frac{h^2}{2x^2} + \frac{h^3}{3x^3} - \&c. \right]$$

$$\therefore \frac{\triangle y}{\triangle x} = \frac{1}{\log_e a} \left[\frac{1}{x} - \frac{h}{2x^2} + \frac{h^2}{3x^3} - \&c. \right]$$

Now when h is very small, all the terms within

brackets, except the first, **may be neglected, for they** are less in absolute value than

$$\frac{h}{2x^2}\left[1 + \frac{h}{x} + \frac{h^2}{x^2} + \&c.\right]$$

$$< \frac{h}{2x^2} \div \left(1 - \frac{h}{x}\right)$$

$$< \frac{h}{2x(x-h)}$$

a quantity vanishing **with** h. Hence, finally, **when** $\triangle y$, $\triangle x$ are both indefinitely **small, we have**

$$\frac{dy}{dx} = \frac{1}{x \log_e a}.$$

It follows **that if** $y = \log_e x$

$$\frac{dy}{dx} = \frac{1}{x}.$$

Now let $y = a^x$. **Here we** shall **content our-**selves **by proceeding as** follows :—

$$x = \log_a y$$

$$\therefore \frac{dx}{dy} = \frac{1}{y(\log_e a} = \frac{1}{a^x \log_e a}$$

$$\text{and } \frac{dy}{dx} = a^x \log_e a.$$

[**There is no objection in** this case to regarding $\frac{dy}{dx}$ **as the reciprocal of** $\frac{dx}{dy}$, however true it may be that $\frac{dy}{dx}$ is to be regarded as a single expression.]

It follows that if $y = e^x$

$$\frac{dy}{dx} = e^x, \text{ also.}$$

We can now differentiate **any** expression we please, however complex. **There is scarcely ever** any room for much ingenuity **in** the choice of methods in differentiating. Still **at** times we find that space **is saved, and** we avoid the **chance of** errors in working, by modifying **our** method of procedure.

Here are a few examples for differentiation :—

1. Let $y = x (a^2 + x^2) \sqrt{a^2 - x^2}$.

Here, proceeding on **the** straightforward course, we get

$$\frac{dy}{dx} = (a^2 + x^2) \sqrt{a^2 - x^2} + 2x^2 \sqrt{a^2 - x^2} - \frac{x^2 (a^2 + x^2)}{\sqrt{a^2 - x^2}}$$

$$= \frac{a^4 - x^4 + 2a^2 x^2 - 2x^4 - a^2 x^2 - x^4}{\sqrt{a^2 - x^2}}$$

$$= \frac{a^4 + a^2 x^2 - 4 x^4}{\sqrt{a^2 - x^2}}$$

But we might have proceeded thus :—

$$\log y = \log x + \log (a^2 + x^2) + \tfrac{1}{2} \log (a^2 - x^2)$$

∴ differentiating with respect to x

$$\frac{1}{y} \cdot \frac{dy}{dx} = \frac{1}{x} + \frac{2x}{a^2 + x^2} - \frac{x}{a^2 - x^2}$$

$$= \frac{a^4 + a^2 x^2 - 4x^4}{x(a^2 + x^2)(a^2 - x^2)}$$

∴ $$\frac{dy}{dx} = \frac{a^4 + a^2 x^2 - 4x^4}{\sqrt{a^2 - x^2}}$$

2. If $y = \log(\log x)$

$$\frac{dy}{dx} = \frac{1}{x}\frac{1}{\log x}$$

3. If $y = \log(\log[\log x])$

$$\frac{dy}{dx} = \frac{1}{x}\frac{1}{\log x} \cdot \frac{1}{\log(\log x)}$$

4. Let $y = a^{x^x}$.

Here we treat x^x as the variable exponent.

∴ $$\frac{dy}{dx} = \log a \cdot a^{x^x} \cdot \frac{d}{dx}(x^x)$$

$$= \log a \cdot a^{x^x}(x\,x^{x-1} + x^x \cdot \log x)$$

$$= \log a \cdot a^{x^x} x^x (1 + \log x).$$

5. If $y = a^{\log x}$

$$\frac{dy}{dx} = \frac{\log a \cdot a^{\log x}}{x}$$

6. If $y = x^{x^x}$

$$\frac{dy}{dx} = \log x \cdot x^{x^x} x^x (1 + \log x) + x^x (x^{x-1})$$

$$= \log x \cdot x^{x^x} x^x (1 + \log x) + x^{x^x} x^{x-1}$$

LESSON X.

OTHER EXAMPLES: MAXIMA AND MINIMA.

We will consider a few more applications of the differential calculus to problems of maxima and minima.

A, B, Fig. 9, is the section of a plane horizontal surface; L, a light vertically above A. If AB = 1 ft., at what height should L be, that the illumination at the point B may be as great as possible?

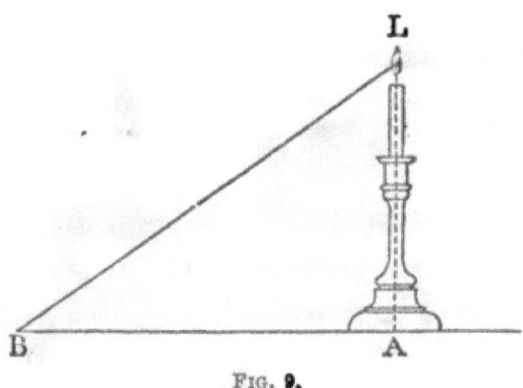

FIG. 9.

[It is clear there is a maximum here, for, if L is in the same level as B, the illumination is zero, and so also the illumination is zero if L is at an infinite height.]

Let $AL = x$. (The light is supposed to be a point, or at any rate to act as if collected at a point.)

Then

$$BL = \sqrt{AB^2 + AL^2}$$
$$= \sqrt{1 + x^2}.$$

And according to the known laws of illumination, the illumination at **B** varies inversely as the square of the distance **BL, and** directly as the sine of the angle **LBA.** Hence, taking m (which will not eventually trouble us) as a suitable constant, we may represent the illumination at **B by** the expression

$$\frac{m}{(BL)^2} \cdot \frac{AL}{BL} = \frac{m \cdot AL}{BL^3}.$$

Call this illumination y; **then**

$$y = \frac{mx}{(1 + x^2)^{\frac{3}{2}}} \quad \cdot \quad \cdot \quad \cdot \quad \cdot \quad \text{(i.)}$$

Now, to differentiate this expression, we take first the differential coefficient of the numerator and multiply it into the denominator. This gives

$$m(1 + x^2)^{\frac{3}{2}}.$$

Then we take negatively the differential coefficient of the denominator and multiply it into the numerator. This gives

$$-\tfrac{3}{2}(1 + x^2)^{\frac{1}{2}} \cdot 2x \times mx, \text{ or } 3(1 + x^2)^{\frac{1}{2}}mx^2.$$

We have only to put the square of the denominator under these two expressions, thus

$$\frac{m(1 + x^2)^{\frac{3}{2}} - 3(1 + x^2)^{\frac{1}{2}}mx^2}{(1 + x^2)^3},$$

to get the differential coefficient of y, and we could reduce and simplify this expression considerably. But observe, we only want to equate the coefficient to zero (that being, as in former cases, the way of getting the required value of x). So that we have no occasion to write out the differential coefficient as above, or to reduce it. We need only write its *numerator* and equate *that* to zero. This gives

$$m(1 + x^2)^{\frac{3}{2}} - 3(1 + x^2)^{\frac{1}{2}}mx^2 = 0 \quad . \quad . \quad \text{(ii.)}$$

or [dividing out by $m(1 + x^2)^{\frac{1}{2}}$]

$$(1 + x^2) = 3x^2.$$

That is

$$2x^2 = 1$$

or

$$x = \frac{1}{\sqrt{2}}.$$

Hence, **AL** should be about $8\frac{2}{5}$ inches.

If we had taken **AB** $= a$ instead of 1, we should have obtained the result

$$a^2 + x^2 = 3x^2;$$

i.e.

$$2x^2 = a^2,$$

or,

$$x = \frac{a}{\sqrt{2}}.$$

Note that the working of this problem would be very short in practice. In fact, after expressing y in terms of x, as at (i.), the student would write down equation (ii.) at once; and solve as above.

Observe, again, that we can vary our method of attacking these problems by varying the relation whose change is to give our maximum. For instance, suppose we attacked the above problem in this wise :—

Let the angle LBA, **Fig. 9**, be called x. Then we know that $BL = BA \sec x$. And the illumination at B may be represented by

$$\frac{m}{BA^2 \sec^2 x} \cdot \sin x.$$

Putting this equal to y, we have

$$y = m \cos^2 x \cdot \sin x.$$

Hence

$$\frac{dy}{dx} = m\left[- 2 \cos x \sin^2 x + \cos^2 x \cos x\right].$$

[I leave the reader to see how this is obtained by applying the rules given in preceding papers, noting that a very moderate degree of practice will enable him to write down such a result at once.]

Equating this expression to zero, we have

$$\cos^2 x \cos x = 2 \cos x \sin^2 x.$$

Hence

$$\frac{\sin^2 x}{\cos^2 x} = \frac{1}{2},$$

or,

$$\tan x = \frac{1}{\sqrt{2}};$$

i.e.

$$\frac{AL}{BA} = \frac{1}{\sqrt{2}}.$$

Hence

$$AL = \frac{BA}{\sqrt{2}} = \frac{1}{\sqrt{2}} \text{ as before.}$$

Neither method has the advantage in this instance, but often a good deal depends on a proper choice of the method to be followed. For example, suppose B is a point on a desk (Fig. 10) sloped at an angle a to the horizon, and that we require the height AL, which will give the maximum illumination in this case. Then the first method would be very inconvenient; but, on applying the second, the value of y is little altered. We only have to put, instead of the factor sin x (*i.e.* sin LBA), the value sin $(x-a)$ [*i.e.* sin LBM], giving

$$y = m \cos^2 x \sin (x - a).$$

And this is differentiated quite as easily as the other expression, giving

$$\frac{1}{m} \cdot \frac{dy}{dx} = -2 \cos x \sin x \sin (x - a)$$
$$+ \cos^2 x \cos (x - a).$$

Equating this to zero, we have

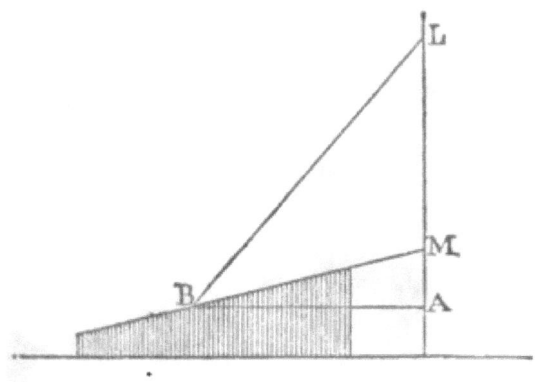

$$2 \cos x \sin x \sin (x - a) = \cos^2 x \cos (x - a),$$

or,

$$2 \sin x \sin (x - a) = \cos x \cos (x - a) \dots \text{(iii.)}$$

Here we want only a moderate familiarity with trigonometrical processes to get out our result, for equation (iii.) is the same as

$$2 \cos a - 2 \cos (2x - a) = \cos a + \cos (2x - a);$$

that is

$$3 \cos (2x - a) = \cos a,$$

or

$$\cos (2x - a) = \frac{\cos a}{3}.$$

This is sufficient for finding x, because a is supposed to be known. Suppose, for example, a is equal to eight degrees, *the slope of my desk*, for I have taken the notion of *working out this particular problem with the practical design of determining how high I should set the moderator which illuminates the paper* **I** *am* *writing* **upon ;** we have then,

$$\cos (2x - 8°) = \tfrac{1}{3} \cos 8°$$
$$= \tfrac{1}{3}(·99027) \begin{cases} \text{from a table of} \\ \text{natural cosines} \end{cases}$$
$$= ·33009$$
$$= \cos (70° \ 44') \text{ nearly enough ;}$$
$$\therefore \ 2x - 8° = 70° \ 44'$$
$$2x = 78° \ 44'$$
$$x = 39° \ 22'.$$

And AL, Fig. 10, is equal to BA tan x. Now, in the case of my desk and light, BA is equal to 18 in., and B, the part of the desk where I actually write (shifting the paper to this point as I write on, line by line) is about 4 in. above the level of the table ; so that the height of the light should be

$$(4 + 18 \tan 39° \ 22') \text{ in.}$$

I take out the log tan of 39° 22′, which is 1·91404, and add to it the logarithm of 18, which is 1·25527, getting 1·16931, which is the logarithm of 14·768. Adding 4 to this, I find that the best height for the light of the moderator (above the surface of the table) is as nearly as possible 18¾ in.

LESSON XI.

VANISHING FRACTIONS.

THE reader has seen enough of the application of the differential calculus to **problems of maxima and minima to** feel satisfied of the **value of** the method. I may now briefly consider **another** class of problems to which the calculus may be conveniently applied.

A differential coefficient is in reality **a** fraction of the form $\frac{0}{0}$, or what is termed a vanishing fraction, **and, like many other vanishing** fractions, **it** has a real value. **Now it is often necessary to find the** value of **vanishing fractions, and though ordinary** algebra may sometimes **be successfully employed for the purpose,** this is **not always possible, and** often, though possible, it is very difficult. **The** differential calculus **enables** us to treat such fractions very simply.

Let us take such a vanishing fraction, and consider what is really required for its evaluation.

Take the fraction

$$\frac{(x^2 - a^2)}{x^3 - a^3},$$

the numerator and denominator of which both vanish when x **is** equal to a. Now we can at once **find** the **value of** this **fraction** by striking out the common factor $x - a$, and so changing it into the form

$$\frac{(x + a)}{x^2 + ax + a^2},$$

the value of which is $\frac{2}{3a}$ when $x = a$. Even to this simple application of algebra there is an objection; since striking out a factor equal to 0 is a questionable process. The result, however, is correct enough.

But the only legitimate way of treating such a fraction would be to inquire what its value is when x is taken very nearly equal to a, as $a + h$, and so trying to find out what value the fraction approaches as x approaches the value a. Let us do this. Our fraction becomes

$$\frac{(a + h)^2 - a^2}{(a + h)^3 - a^3} = \frac{2ah + h^2}{3a^2h + 3ah^2 + h^3} = \frac{2a + h}{3a^2 + 3ah + h^2}.$$

Here we can see at once that by making h small enough we can get our fraction as near as we please to $\frac{2a}{3a^2} \left(i.e.\ \text{to}\ \frac{2}{3a} \right)$ in value; and we therefore conclude that $\frac{2}{3a}$ is the value when h is 0, or when x is equal to a. But a little consideration will show the reader that this process corresponds exactly to that for obtaining the differential coefficient both of the numerator and denominator. Hence, he will be prepared to find that when we have a fraction of the form $\frac{u}{y}$, where both the expressions u and y involve x, and both vanish for a certain value of x, **the fraction may** be evaluated by simply writing **for u** its differential coefficient $\frac{du}{dx}$, and for y **its** differential coefficient $\frac{dy}{dx}$.

Take, **for** instance, the expression

$$\frac{x-1}{x^6-1},$$

which assumes **the form** $\frac{0}{0}$ when $x=1$. Following the rule, we write for a new numerator the differential coefficient of $x-1$, *i.e.* 1, **and** for a new denominator the differential **coefficient** of x^6-1, *i.e.* $6x^5$.

Our fraction thus becomes

$$\frac{1}{6x^5},$$

which **has the** value $\frac{1}{6}$ when $x=1$.

But it may happen that **the** new fraction **thus** formed is itself a vanishing fraction. In this **case** we must repeat **the** process until we obtain **a fraction** which is not indeterminate in form.

Thus, suppose **we** have the fraction

$$\frac{(x-1)^3}{x^6-3x^5+3x^4-3x^2+3x-1},$$

which is **of** the form $\frac{0}{0}$ when $x=1$. We apply the rule, getting

$$\frac{3(x-1)^2}{6x^5-15x^4+12x^3-6x+3},$$

which is still of the form $\frac{0}{0}$. Again applying the rule, we get

$$\frac{3 \cdot 2 \cdot (x-1)}{30x^4 - 60x^3 + 36x^2 - 6},$$

which is still of the form $\frac{0}{0}$. Lastly, applying the rule yet once more, we get

$$\frac{3 \cdot 2 \cdot 1}{120x^3 - 180x^2 + 72x}.$$

And when $x = 1$, this fraction has the value

$$\frac{6}{120 - 180 + 72} = \frac{6}{12} = \frac{1}{2}.$$

Other vanishing fractions may be similarly treated; and this application of the differential calculus thus becomes of great utility.

LESSON XII.

TANGENTS TO CURVES.

I PROPOSE now to give two geometrical illustrations
of a differential coefficient, which, when their nature
is rightly understood, and especially the circumstance
that the various values of a function can *always* be
expressed by means of a curve, will be found of great
value in indicating the real meaning at once of
differentiation and integration.

Let O, Fig. 11, be the origin, OX and OY, at right
angles to each other, the axes of *x* and *y*.

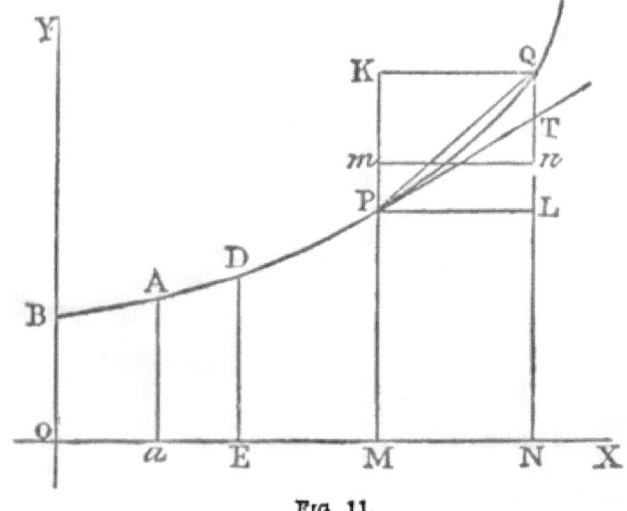

FIG. 11.

Then the *x* we have been dealing with—our inde-
pendent variable—may be regarded as measured along

OX; and y, the dependent variable, along OY. So that when we write $y = f(x)$, *i.e.* y is such and such a function of x, we may represent any values of x by OM, ON along OX, calculate the resulting values of y, and set up corresponding lines MP, NQ parallel to OY. If we suppose this done for all values of x, we get in every case a curve such as is supposed to be shown in part by APQ, the ordinates MP, NQ, &c., representing the values of y corresponding to the values of x represented by the abscissæ OM, ON, &c., respectively.

Supposing, then, that when $x = $ OM, $y = $ MP, we may take MN to represent a finite increment of x or Δx, and get NQ for the corresponding value of y. Draw PL parallel to OX, cutting off NL = PM from QN, this new value of y—that is from $y + \Delta y$. Then PL $= \Delta x$ and QL $= \Delta y$. And what we have represented by

$$\frac{\Delta y}{\Delta x}$$

is the ratio **QL** : PL, or the tangent of the angle QPL, when PQ is a secant line. If now we imagine N brought **nearer** and nearer to PM, it is manifest that the secant **line** PQ draws nearer and nearer in position to the tangent line PT, and the ratio QL : **PL** approaches nearer and nearer in value to the ratio **TL** : PL, the trigonometrical **tangent** of the angle which the geometrical tangent to the curve APQ at P makes **with** the axis of x. Hence the differential coefficient $\dfrac{dy}{dx}$ represents the tangent of the angle TPT.

Here we have at once an illustration of the geometrical meaning of a differential coefficient and a useful application of the differential calculus. The reader of elementary treatises on plane co-ordinate geometry knows how important a process is the

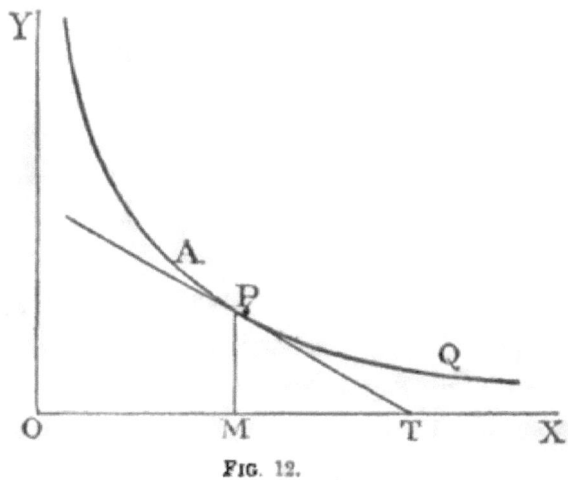

Fig. 12.

determination of the equation to the tangent at a given point of a curve, and how cumbrous is the method which has to be employed for its determination by elementary methods. With the differential calculus the process is simplicity itself.

Thus, suppose APQ is a part of the rectangular hyperbola whose equation is

$$xy = a^2,$$

and that we require the equation to the tangent PT at a point P, whose ordinates are $OM = x_1$ and $PM = y_1$. We have

$$y = \frac{a^2}{x}; \quad \frac{dy}{dx} = -\frac{a^2}{x^2},$$

whence

$$\tan PTX = -\frac{a^2}{x_1{}^2},$$

and the equation to PT is, therefore,

$$\frac{y - y_1}{x - x_1} = -\frac{a^2}{x_1{}^2} = -\frac{y_1}{x_1},$$

or,

$$x_1 y + y_1 x = 2x_1 y_1 = 2a^2.$$

Again, the equation to the ellipse with origin at centre and major axis as axis of x, is

$$\frac{x^2}{a^2} + \frac{y^2}{b^2} = 1,$$

or,

$$y = \frac{b}{a}\sqrt{a^2 - x^2}; \quad \frac{dy}{dx} = -\frac{b}{a}\frac{x}{\sqrt{a^2 - x^2}}.$$

Wherefore the equation to the tangent at a point x_1, y_1, on the curve is

$$\frac{y - y_1}{x - x_1} = -\frac{b}{a}\frac{x_1}{\sqrt{a^2 - x_1{}^2}} = -\frac{b^2 x_1}{a^2 y_1},$$

or,

$$a^2 y_1 y + b^2 x_1 x = a^2 y_1{}^2 + b^2 x_1{}^2 = a^2 b^2,$$

i.e.

$$\frac{y_1 y}{a^2} + \frac{x_1 x}{b^2} = 1.$$

LESSON XIII.

AREAS OF CURVES.

NEXT take the following illustration of a differential coefficient, which is in many respects more important still than that last considered.

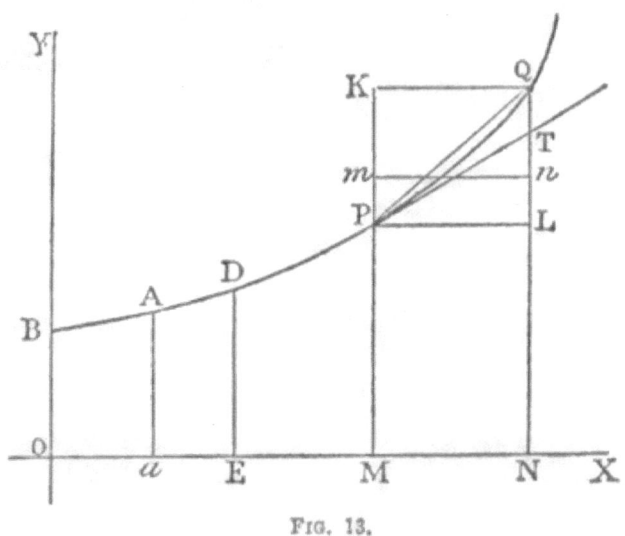

FIG. 13.

Instead of taking for the dependent variable the ordinate of a curve, take the area, *a*APM (Fig. 13), measured from some fixed ordinate A*a* to the ordinate PM corresponding to the varying value of the absciss OM or *x*.

Putting $MN = \Delta x$, we have, if

$$u = \text{area } APMa$$
$$u + \Delta u = \text{area } AQNa$$
$$\Delta u = \text{area } MPQN$$
$$\therefore \quad \frac{\Delta u}{\Delta x} = \frac{\text{area } MPQN}{MN}$$

$=$ side nN of a rect. mN equal to $MPQN$.

Now manifestly the smaller MN is taken the nearer is the rectangle PN in area to $MPQN$; it is not merely that the difference, the area PQL (PQ curved) is absolutely less, but it manifestly bears a constantly diminishing ratio to the area PN; until finally, when MN is taken small enough, this ratio will be a vanishing one. Hence, while

$$\frac{\Delta u}{\Delta x} = nN,$$

we manifestly have

$$\frac{du}{dx} = PM = y,$$

or the differential coefficient of the area between a curve, the axis of x, a fixed ordinate, and the variable ordinate, is this last-named ordinate. Here the language and notation of differentials are, I think, simpler and more natural than those belonging to the method of coefficients. We should say simply du the differential of the area, that is the small increment of the area, is equal to ydx, that is to the area contained by y and dx the differential of x; which is the same as saying that, ultimately, the area PQNM = rectangle PN.

But now notice the power we have obtained for determining not only areas of surfaces bounded by curved lines, but also any function which might be symbolised by such areas. When we have written of any such area as APMa, or of any function which may be represented by such an area, the relation

$$\frac{du}{dx} = y,$$

where y is some function of x, we can tell at once what u is, if only we can determine what function has y for its differential coefficient. For we have seen that no two quantities can have the same differential coefficient, unless either they are equal or differ only by a constant. (Geometrically this is much the same as saying that no other area but APMa has PM, the ordinate of the curve APQ, for the measure of its rate of increase, except some area, as OBPM, EDPM, or the like, differing from aAPM by some quantity which remains constant while we vary OM and with it PM.)

Now, although determining what quantity that is which has some given function for its differential coefficient is by no means so easy or so sure a process as differentiating, yet in a great number of cases this process, which is called *integration*, can be readily managed; in others it can be accomplished with more or less difficulty; and in yet others, approximations can be made to the desired integration, and the result we require can be determined with all necessary approach to exactitude.

The notation for the converse process to differentiation, or integration, is as follows :—When we have a function u such that

$$\frac{du}{dx} = y,$$

we express the same relation by saying that

$$u = \int y dx.$$

To be more precise we may write

$$u = \int y dx + \text{a constant,}$$

but the constant is in reality understood in the other form of expression.

A geometrical illustration of the equation

$$u = \int y dx,$$

may be found thus :

Let APQ, Fig. 14, be a curve as before,
OM $= x$, PM $= y$, M$n = \Delta x$.

Then the area AQNa is the sum of a number of small

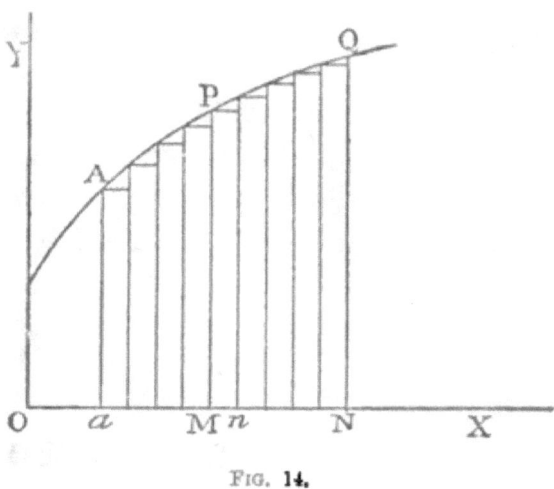

FIG. 14.

rectangles like Pn, when these are made indefinitely
thin. Now

$$Pn = y\Delta x.$$

Therefore the statement

$$\text{area (or } u) = \int y\,dx,$$

may be taken to mean that we get the area between
AQ, OX, and certain boundary ordinates, by summing a multitude of very thin rectangles like Pn
between the corresponding ordinates. This is an
indefinite statement; and $\int y\,dx$ is called an indefinite integral. When we take definite limiting
ordinates as Aa, QN, corresponding to $x = Oa$, and

$x =$ ON (say $x = a$ and $x = b$, respectively), we get the definite **area AQN**a; and we write

$$\text{area AQN}a = \int_a^b y\,dx,$$

which means that from the value of $\int y\,dx$ when b is written for x, **is** to be subtracted the **value** when a is written **for** x, to give the area of the space between **the** ordinates corresponding to these values.

Be it noticed that what we have here said about areas applies to any quantities which may be represented by areas, **and therefore** practically to any quantities whatsoever. If we can obtain an expression for the small increment of any quantity u corresponding to any small increment of the variable, and can ascertain by any process what quantity that is which has such an increment, we can determine u by the process of integration.

Examples **will,** however, **best show the value of** all this.

LESSON XIV.

USE OF THE INTEGRAL CALCULUS.

HERE are a few simple examples of the application of the integral calculus as explained in the last lesson :—

OPB is a parabola, OX its axis, the equation to the parabola being $y^2 = mx$. To determine the area OBM, when OM = b.

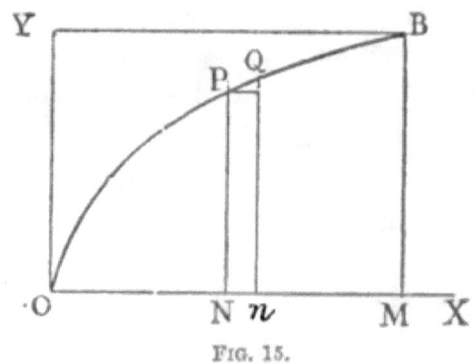

FIG. 15.

Draw ordinates PN, Qn close together. Let ON = x, Nn = Δx. Rectangle Pn = $y\Delta x$. Then, since the area is the sum of all such rectangles as Pn between OM and BM when they are made indefinitely thin, we have

$$\text{area OBM} = \int_0^b y\,dx$$

$$= \int_0^b \sqrt{mx}\,dx.$$

We have to find out what expression that is which has $\sqrt{mx}$ for its differential coefficient. We may write this $\sqrt{m}.x^{\frac{1}{2}}$; and we know that in differentiating x raised to any power, the index sinks by unity and appears also as a factor in the differential coefficient. Therefore $x^{\frac{1}{2}}$ must be the differential coefficient of $x^{\frac{3}{2}}$ multiplied by a factor which is altered into unity when multiplied by $\frac{3}{2}$; that is to say, the factor must be $\frac{2}{3}$. Hence

$$\int \sqrt{mx}\, dx = \sqrt{m}.\tfrac{2}{3}x^{\frac{3}{2}} + \text{a constant.}$$

(The student should differentiate this expression to make sure that its differential coefficient is $\sqrt{mx}$.)

Giving to x first the value b, and then the value 0, we find

$$\text{area OBM} = \frac{2\sqrt{mb^3}}{3} + C - (0 + C) = \frac{2\sqrt{mb^3}}{3},$$

or, since $OM = b$, and $BM = \sqrt{mb}$;

$$\text{area OBM} = \tfrac{2}{3}\text{ rect. BO.}$$

Of course, there is no occasion, in practice, for all that has been here written out.

Take another case, to show how such problems are dealt with :—

Required the volume of the right cone produced

G

by the revolution of the right triangle OBM, Fig. 16,
around OM : OM = a, BM = b.

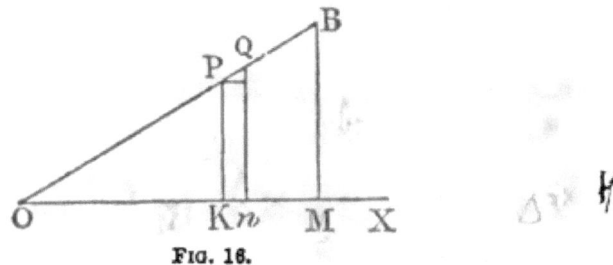

FIG. 16.

Put $OK = x$, $Kn = \Delta x$. Then the volume produced by the revolution of the rect. Pn around
$OX = \pi\,(PK)^2 . Kn.$

$$= \pi \left(\frac{b}{a}\right)^2 x^2 \Delta x\,;$$

$\therefore$ required volume $= \dfrac{\pi b^2}{a^2}\displaystyle\int_0^a x^2\,dx.$

Now obviously the expression of which x^2 is
the differential coefficient is $\frac{1}{3}x^3 +$ const. (Differentiate and see.)   Hence

volume of cone $= \dfrac{\pi b^2}{3a^2} . a^3 = \dfrac{1}{3}\pi a b^2.$

Suppose the following problem set :—

In the cone last considered the density of successive
thin circles such as the one formed by the revolution of
Pn varies as the square of OK; required the mass
of the cone formed by the revolution of OBM.

Proceeding as before, we find the mass produced by the revolution of Pn around OX

$$= \pi \left(\frac{b}{a}\right)^2 x^2 \Delta x \times \rho x^2,$$

where ρ is the density at a unit of distance from O along OX. Hence in this case

$$\text{Mass req.} = \pi \left(\frac{b}{a}\right)^2 \rho \int_0^a x^4 dx = \frac{\pi \rho}{5} \left(\frac{b}{a}\right)^2 a^5 = \frac{1}{5} \pi \rho a^3 b^2.$$

These examples are only intended to give an idea of the use of integration; in more advanced study the student will recognise the principles by which areas, volumes, masses, lengths, and arcs, &c., are determined. Let it suffice, in this preliminary view, to note how problems which, dealt with geometrically, would require more or less skill or artifice, can be dealt with easily and systematically by integration.

LESSON XV.

DIRECT INTEGRATION.

We have next to consider the various methods available for integrating the different expressions which come before us when we apply the methods of the integral calculus.

First, some expressions can be integrated at once, because they have been already obtained as the differential coefficients of known functions. For these the following table, which gives all the differential coefficients of simple functions, will be found useful, and should always be held in the student's remembrance. We write

$$\frac{d}{dx} \text{ (function of } x)$$

for the differential coefficient of the function with respect to x.

Since

Differential Coefficient	Deduced Integral
$\frac{d}{dx}(x^n) = nx^{n-1}$;	$\int x^n dx = \dfrac{x^{n+1}}{n+1}$
$\frac{d}{dx}(\log_e x) = \dfrac{1}{x}$;	$\int \dfrac{dx}{x} = \log_e x$
$\frac{d}{dx}(\log_a x) = \dfrac{1}{x \log_e a}$;	$\int \dfrac{dx}{x} = \log_e a \,.\, \log_a x = \log_e x$

$$\frac{d}{dx}(e^x) = e^x;$$

$$\int e^x dx = e^x$$

$$\frac{d}{dx}(a^x) = a^x \cdot \log_e a;$$

$$\int a^x dx = \frac{a^x}{\log_e a}$$

$$\frac{d}{dx}(\sin x) = \cos x;$$

$$\int \cos x \, dx = \sin x$$

$$\frac{d}{dx}(\cos x) = -\sin x;$$

$$\int \sin x \, dx = -\cos x$$

$$\frac{d}{dx}(\tan x) = \frac{1}{\cos^2 x};$$

$$\int \frac{dx}{\cos^2 x} = \tan x$$

$$\frac{d}{dx}(\cot x) = -\frac{1}{\sin^2 x};$$

$$\int \frac{dx}{\sin^2 x} = -\cot x$$

$$\frac{d}{dx}(\sec x) = \frac{\sin x}{\cos^2 x};$$

$$\int \frac{\sin x \, dx}{\cos^2 x} = \sec x$$

$$\frac{x}{dx}(\operatorname{cosec} x) = -\frac{\cos x}{\sin^2 x};$$

$$\int \frac{\cos x \, dx}{\sin^2 x} = -\operatorname{cosec} x$$

$$\frac{d}{dx}\left(\sin^{-1}\frac{x}{a}\right) = \frac{1}{\sqrt{a^2 - x^2}};$$

$$\int \frac{dx}{\sqrt{a^2 - x^2}} = \sin^{-1}\frac{x}{a}$$

$$\frac{d}{dx}\left(\cos^{-1}\frac{x}{a}\right) = -\frac{1}{\sqrt{a^2 - x^2}};$$

$$\int \frac{dx}{\sqrt{a^2 - x^2}} = -\cos^{-1}\frac{x}{a}$$

$$\frac{d}{dx}\left(\tan^{-1}\frac{x}{a}\right) = \frac{a}{a^2 + x^2};$$

$$\int \frac{dx}{a^2 + x^2} = \frac{1}{a}\tan^{-1}\frac{x}{a}$$

$$\frac{d}{dx}\left(\cot^{-1}\frac{x}{a}\right) = -\frac{a}{a^2 + x^2};$$

$$\int \frac{dx}{a^2 + x^2} = -\frac{1}{a}\cot^{-1}\frac{x}{a}$$

$$\frac{d}{dx}\left(\sec^{-1}\frac{x}{a}\right) = \frac{a}{x\sqrt{x^2 - a^2}};$$

$$\int \frac{dx}{x\sqrt{x^2 - a^2}} = \frac{1}{a}\sec^{-1}\frac{x}{a}$$

$$\frac{d}{dx}\left(\operatorname{cosec}^{-1}\right) = -\frac{a}{x\sqrt{x^2 - a^2}};$$

$$\int \frac{dx}{x\sqrt{x^2 - a^2}} = -\frac{1}{a}\operatorname{cosec}^{-1}\frac{x}{a}$$

The last six relations are, of course, reducible to three only, so far as integration is concerned. For, since $\sin^{-1}\dfrac{x}{a} + \cos^{-1}\dfrac{x}{a} = \tan^{-1}\dfrac{x}{a} + \cot^{-1}\dfrac{x}{a}$

$$= \sec^{-1}\dfrac{x}{a} + \operatorname{cosec}^{-1}\dfrac{x}{a} = \dfrac{\pi}{2},$$

it is manifest that the second values given respectively to

$$\int \frac{dx}{\sqrt{a^2 - x^2}}, \int \frac{dx}{a^2 + x^2}, \text{ and } \int \frac{dx}{x\sqrt{x^2 - a^2}},$$

differ from the first only by a constant, to wit, $\dfrac{\pi}{2}$ in the first of the three cases, and $\dfrac{\pi}{2a}$ in the other three cases.

LESSON XVI.

INTEGRATION BY SUBSTITUTION.

It is sometimes found that an expression which cannot be integrated as it stands may be integrated by changing the variable. The best way of making clear the rules for doing this will be by considering a simple geometrical example.

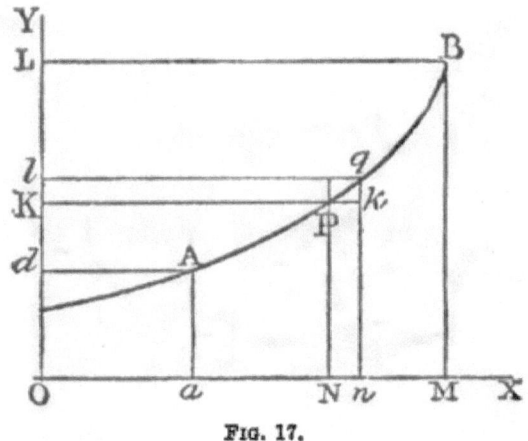

FIG. 17.

Suppose we want to determine the area APBMa, Fig. 17, which, as we have seen, is represented by

$$\int_a^b y\,dx.$$

(Suppositions the same as before.) Then drawing Ad, BL, perpendicular to OY, we might find it convenient to regard y as the dependent variable, passing from Od to OL, instead of taking x from Oa to OM. As before, we should get for our element of area Pn; where Nn is $\triangle x$, a small increment of x. We can, however, as readily use lK, or $\triangle y$, the corresponding increment of y. For we have

$$N n = P k = \frac{Pk}{qk} \cdot qk = \frac{\triangle x}{\triangle y} \cdot \triangle y.$$

That is

$$\text{rect. } P n = \mathbf{PN} \cdot Pk = y\frac{\triangle x}{\triangle y} \cdot \triangle y;$$

or ultimately when $\triangle x$, $\triangle y$ are made indefinitely small,

$$P n = y\frac{dx}{dy} \cdot dy,$$

and taking y from Od ($= a_1$ suppose) to OL ($= b_1$ suppose) we have

$$\text{area ABM}a = \int_{a_1}^{b_1} y\frac{dx}{dy} \cdot dy.$$

In any such case, when we have to integrate the expression $\int u dx$, between $x = a$ and $x = b$, where u is some function of x, we may regard x as a function of some new variable y, if only by changing y between certain limits a_1 and b_1 we get all the values of u which it would receive when we changed x between a and b. We have then

$$u\,dx = u\frac{dx}{dy} \cdot dy \text{ and } \int_a^b u\,dx = \int_{a_1}^{b_1} u\frac{dx}{dy} \cdot dy,$$

and the work of integration is reduced to that of integrating the indefinite integral

$$\int u\frac{dx}{dy} \cdot dy.$$

Suppose, for example, we had to integrate

$$\int \frac{dx}{x\sqrt{x^2 - a^2}}.$$

Let us try the experiment of putting

$$x = \frac{1}{y}.$$

Then

$$\frac{dx}{dy} = -\frac{1}{y^2} \text{ and } \int \frac{dx}{x\sqrt{x^2 - a^2}} = \int \frac{y^2}{\sqrt{1 - a^2 y^2}}\left(-\frac{1}{y^2}\right) dy$$

$$= -\int \frac{dy}{\sqrt{1 - a^2 y^2}} = -\frac{1}{a}\int \frac{dy}{\sqrt{\frac{1}{a^2} - y^2}}$$

$$= -\frac{1}{a}\sin^{-1} ay = -\frac{1}{a}\sin^{-1}\frac{a}{x}.$$

Again, take

$$\int \frac{dx}{x\sqrt{2ax - a^2}}.$$

Here noting that the denominator may be written

$$x\sqrt{x^2 - (x-a)^2},$$

we are led to try putting

$$\frac{x - a}{x} = z,$$

which will obviously simplify the radical. This gives

$$1 - \frac{a}{x} = z, \text{ or } x = \frac{a}{1-z}; \frac{dx}{dz} = \frac{a}{(1-z)^2} = \frac{x^2}{a};$$

and

$$\frac{x^2 - (x-a)^2}{x^2} = 1 - z^2,$$

i.e.

$$\sqrt{2ax - x^2} = x\sqrt{1 - z^2};$$

$$\therefore \int \frac{dx}{x\sqrt{2ax - x^2}} = \int \frac{1}{x^2\sqrt{1 - z^2}} \frac{dx}{dz} . dz = \frac{1}{a}\int \frac{dz}{\sqrt{1 - z^2}}$$

$$= \frac{1}{a} \sin^{-1} z = \frac{1}{a} \sin^{-1} \frac{x - a}{x}.$$

This method of integration by substitution is usually tentative—several substitutions may be tried before one is hit upon which gives an integrable expression.

LESSON XVII.

INTEGRATION BY PARTS.

ANOTHER method (also tentative) is available when we are endeavouring to integrate an expression.

Supposing we had to obtain the area ABMa. (Fig. 17, p. 87.) We might in some cases find it more convenient to determine, instead, the area ABLd, which gives us what we are seeking, because

area ABMa = rect. LM − rect. da − area ABLd.

If we regard ON, PN (or PK, PN), the ordinates of P, as functions x and y of some third variable t, then we have

rect. KN = xy = u, say ;

and if we increase t by Δt so that x becomes On or $x + \Delta x$, and y becomes Ol or $y + \Delta y$, we have : increase of rect. KN ultimately

= rect. Pn + rect. lP ;

that is,

$$\Delta (xy) = y \Delta x + x \Delta y$$
$$= y \frac{\Delta x}{\Delta t} \Delta t + x \frac{\Delta y}{\Delta t} \Delta t,$$

whence, making Δt indefinitely small,

$$\frac{d(xy)}{dt} = y\frac{dx}{dt} + x\frac{dy}{dt},$$

or

$$xy = \int y\,\frac{dx}{dt}\,dt + \int x\,\frac{dy}{dt}\,dt;$$

(This really corresponds only to saying that in passing from P to B, the increment of rect. KN, namely the gnomon LPM, is equal to the sum of the increments of the areas APNa and APKd.)

Wherefore

$$\int x\,\frac{dy}{dt}\,dt = xy - \int y\,\frac{dx}{dt}\,dt.$$

Thus if an integral can be written in the form

$$\int x\,\frac{dy}{dt}\,dt,$$

where x and y are both functions of t, we may substitute for the integral so written

$$xy - \int y\,\frac{dx}{dt}\,dt.$$

This is equivalent to finding the area ABLd, instead of the area ABMa.

As an example consider the integral

$$\int \log x\,dx.$$

This may be written

$$\int \frac{dx}{dx} \cdot \log x\,dx.$$

Hence by the formula just obtained we have

$$\int \log x \, dx = x \log x - \int x \cdot \frac{1}{x} \, dx$$
$$= x \log x - x.$$

When the student tries the method of integrating by parts, he will often find that though he cannot at once integrate the modified expression, he has made a measurable advance towards a directly integrable form. In such cases he may see his way to a further advance on repeating the integration by parts, and eventually to complete integration. Such a process is called integration by reduction.

The student will also note early that many functions which can be resolved into partial fractions may be directly integrated in that form.

In more advanced treatises on the differential and integral calculus these methods are described in detail.

LESSON XVIII.

USEFUL INTEGRALS.

I PROPOSE now to consider certain useful integrals which may be obtained by the processes already described. I shall treat them in a rather novel manner, though there will be nothing new in the matter presented.

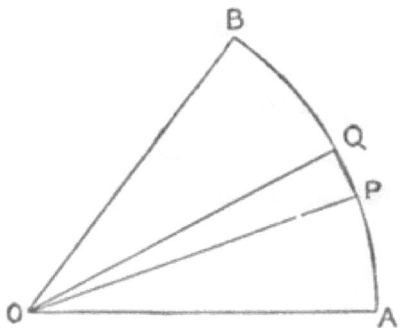

FIG. 18.—AREA OF A CIRCULAR SECTOR.

Let AB (Fig. 18) be a circular arc round the centre O, and let it be required to determine the area of the sector AOB, where $AO = r$ and $\angle AOB = a$.

Let PQ be a small element of the arc AB. Let $\angle AOP = \theta$; $\angle QOP = \Delta\theta$.

Then if QP be joined,

the triangle $QOP = OP \cdot OQ \sin QOP$

$$= \frac{r^2}{2} \sin \Delta\theta.$$

And when $\Delta\theta$ becomes $d\theta$, or is made indefinitely small,

$\sin \Delta\theta = \Delta\theta$, and the triangle $QOP = r^2 d\theta$.

Hence, since the area AOB is manifestly equal in the limit to the sum of all such triangles as QOP in the sector, when their number becomes infinite, we have

$$\text{Sector } AOB = \tfrac{1}{2}\int_0^a r^2 d\theta = \frac{r^2}{2}\int_o^a d\theta.$$

Now we know that

$$\int d\theta = \theta + C,$$

where C is some constant (which need not trouble us). Therefore—

$$\text{Sector } AOB = \frac{r^2}{2}\left(a + C - \overline{0 + C}\right) = \frac{r^2}{2}\cdot a.$$

That is, the area of a sector is represented numerically by half the product of the numbers representing r the length of the radius, and ra the length of the circular arc.

Observe that we learn nothing new from this application of the integral calculus. It does not tell us what the length of the arc is; nor is anything derived from the calculus in the recognition of the relation between the area on the one hand

and the arc and radius on the other. When we
take $a = 2\pi$ so as to get the whole circle, we find
that the area of the circle is represented by the
product of the radius and the circumference.[1] But
our process has not squared the circle for us ; for
it has not shown the length of the circumference,
or of the arc AB in the particular case dealt
with.

It is only because we *know* the lengths of
circular arcs that our result is really a determination
of the area of the sector.

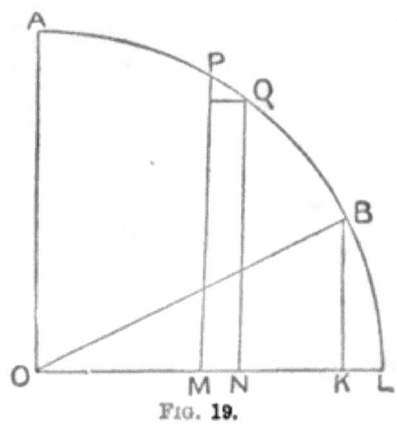

Fig. 19.

---

[1] I write thus for shortness. As a matter of fact, an area
can no more be represented by the product of two lengths
than a period of time can be represented by a number
of acres, or the content of a solid by a number of hours.
Such an expression as the above means only that, certain
units being taken, the relation indicated exists between the
numbers mentioned. Thus, if we say that the area of a rectangle
is represented by the product of its sides, we mean really that if
a square on the unit of length is taken as the unit of area, then
the area of a rectangle is represented numerically by the product
of the numbers representing the lengths of two adjacent sides.

Suppose, now, we **wish** to determine by means of the integral calculus the area OABK (Fig. 19), where ABL is a quadrant.

We have already determined the area in what precedes; for, joining OB, we know the area of the sector AOB, and adding thereto the triangle OBK, we have the total area OABK.

Thus if radius OA $= a$, OK $= x_1$, then

$$BK = \sqrt{a^2 - x_1^2};$$

and arc AB $= a \sin^{-1}\left(\dfrac{x_1}{a}\right).$

Hence, area OABK = triangle OBK + sect. AOB

$$= \frac{x_1 \sqrt{a^2 - x_1^2}}{2} + \frac{a^2}{2} \sin^{-1}\left(\frac{x_1}{a}\right).$$

But suppose we **wish to determine** the area OABK independently, **by the** summation of such rectangular strips as QM, made in the limit indefinitely narrow.

We put OM $= x$, MN $= \Delta x$. Thus **we have**

Rect. QM $= \sqrt{a^2 - x^2}\, \Delta x$; and area **OABK** = sum of all such rectangles made **infinite in** number, and so taken indefinitely thin, between OA where $x = 0$, and BK where $x = x_1$.

Thus area OABK $= \displaystyle\int_0^{x_1} \sqrt{a^2 - x^2}\, dx.$

Now, to integrate

$$\sqrt{a^2 - x^2}\, dx,$$

we may try the method of integration by parts, noticing that unity is the differential coefficient of x with respect to x. **Thus**

$$\int \sqrt{a^2 - x^2}\, dx = \int \frac{dx}{dx} \sqrt{a^2 - x^2}\, dx$$

$$= x\sqrt{a^2 - x^2} - \int x \frac{d}{dx}\sqrt{a^2 - x^2}\, dx$$

$$= x\sqrt{a^2 - x^2} + \int \frac{x^2\, dx}{\sqrt{a^2 - x^2}}. \qquad (1)$$

But here we notice that

$$\frac{x^2}{\sqrt{a^2 - x^2}} = \frac{x^2 - a^2 + a^2}{\sqrt{a^2 - x^2}}$$

$$= -\sqrt{a^2 - x^2} + \frac{a^2}{\sqrt{a^2 - x^2}}.$$

So that

$$\int \frac{x^2\, dx}{\sqrt{a^2 - x^2}} = -\int \sqrt{a^2 - x^2}\, dx + a^2 \int \frac{dx}{\sqrt{a^2 - x^2}} \qquad (2)$$

the first part of which, when written in equation 1, will clearly give us what can be conveniently taken over to the other side with a positive sign, while the other part is in our table of known integrals at p. 85. Thus, substituting in (1) from (2) and transposing, we get

$$2 \int \sqrt{a^2 - x^2}\, dx = x\sqrt{a^2 - x^2} + a^2 \int \frac{dx}{\sqrt{a^2 - x^2}}$$

$$= x\sqrt{a^2 - x^2} + a^2 \sin^{-1}\frac{x}{a};$$

or,

$$\int \sqrt{a^2 - x^2}\, dx = \frac{x\sqrt{a^2 - x^2}}{2} + \frac{a^2}{2} \sin^{-1}\frac{x}{a}.$$

Putting 0 for x in this, we get 0 ; so that

$$\int_0^{x_1} \sqrt{a^2 - x^2}\, dx = \frac{x_1 \sqrt{a^2 - x_1^2}}{2} + \frac{a^2}{2} \sin^{-1} \frac{x_1}{a}.$$

This, therefore, is the required area OABK.

Remembering that this **area** OABK can be divided into the triangle OBK and the sector AOB, we have a ready means of *remembering* as well as of *interpreting* the important relation

$$\int \sqrt{a^2 - x^2}\, dx = \frac{x\sqrt{x^2 - x^2}}{2} + \frac{a^2}{2} \sin^{-1} \frac{x}{a}.$$

We have given the solution for this integral much as it might be found out by one seeking it without a knowledge of the book method. Having found it, we can conveniently write the solution thus :

$$\int \sqrt{a^2 - x^2}\, dx = x\sqrt{a^2 - x^2} + \int \frac{x^2 dx}{\sqrt{a^2 - x^2}},$$

Also

$$\int \sqrt{a^2 - x^2}\, dx = \int \frac{a^2 - x^2}{\sqrt{a^2 - x^2}} dx = \int \frac{a^2 dx}{\sqrt{a^2 - x^2}} - \int \frac{x^2 dx}{\sqrt{a^2 - x^2}}$$

∴ adding

$$2\int \sqrt{a^2 - x^2}\, dx = x\sqrt{a^2 - x^2} + \int \frac{a^2 dx}{\sqrt{a^2 - x^2}},$$

i.e.

$$\int \sqrt{a^2 - x^2}\, dx = \frac{x\sqrt{a^2 - x^2}}{2} + \frac{a^2}{2} \sin^{-1} \frac{x}{a}.$$

But the student who really wants to understand what he is doing should work out such results in some such way as he would in actual practice, not follow simply the conveniently abridged methods which are formed *after* a result has been obtained.

LESSON XIX.

ELLIPTIC AND HYPERBOLIC INTEGRALS.

THE study of the integral dealt with in our last, in its relation to the area of circular sections (whether sector, segment, or otherwise), leads naturally to the discussion of the areas of other conic sections.

The ellipse, however, requires no new application of the integral calculus. Thus, if BQA, Fig. 20, is a right elliptical quadrant, C the centre of the ellipse,

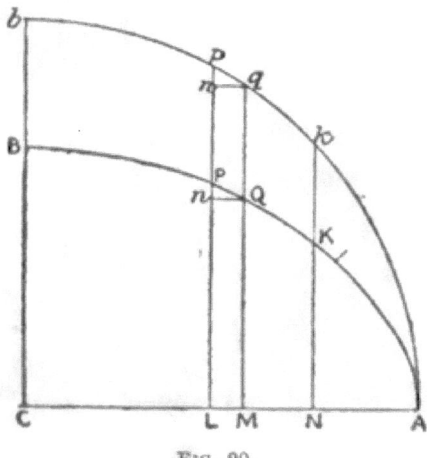

FIG. 20.

and the semi-axes CA and BC are a and b respectively, we know that, putting CL $= x$ and PL $= y$,

$$y^2 = \frac{b^2}{a^2}(a^2 - x^2),$$

and the area of the elementary rectangle QL

$$= ydx = \frac{b}{a}\sqrt{a^2 - x^2}\, dx.$$

So that the area CBKN, in which $CN = x_1$,

$$= \frac{b}{a}\int_0^{x_1} \sqrt{a^2 - x^2}\, dx$$

$$= \frac{b}{a}\left[\frac{x_1\sqrt{a^2 - x_1^2}}{2} + \frac{a^2}{2}\sin^{-1}\frac{x_1}{a} \right]$$

$$= \frac{b}{a}\text{ area } CbkN.$$

When we turn to the hyperbola, however, we find ourselves led to a new integral, and a new application of the integral calculus. (In passing, I wish the reader to notice that my chief object in going over thus the discussion of the simpler integrals, and those more commonly employed, is to associate this part of the student's reading with the actual application of the calculus.)

If KPAR, Fig. 21, is part of a rectangular hyperbola, A the vertex, C the centre, and CZ, CZ′ the asymptotes; and if $CL = x$, $PL = y$, we know that

$$y^2 = x^2 - a^2$$

(where $CA = a$) and taking an ordinate KN, we have the area of an elementary rectangle PM

$$= ydx = \sqrt{x^2 - a^2}\, dx,$$

so that the area AKN, in which $CN = x_1$,

$$= \int_a^{x_1} \sqrt{x^2 - a^2} \, dx,$$

to determine which we must integrate

$$\sqrt{x^2 - a^2} \, dx,$$

not as yet among the quantities **whose** integral **is** known **to us. Before** trying to do **this, let us** con-

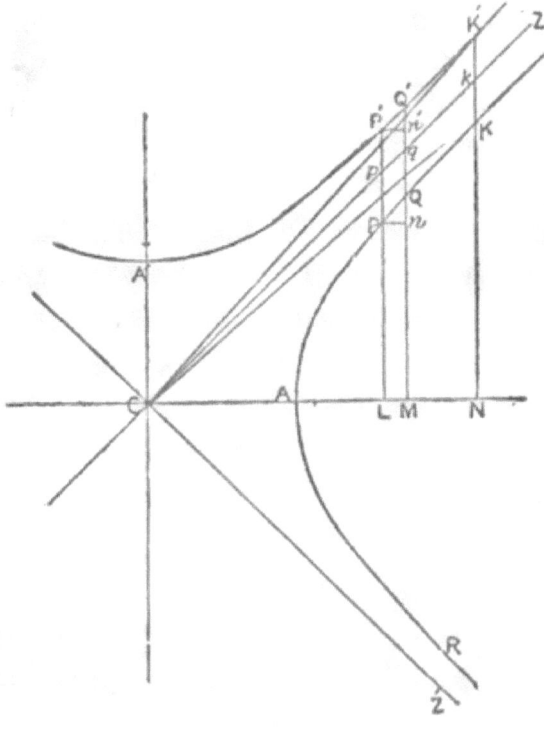

FIG. 21.

sider the conjugate hyperbola $A'P'Q'$. Here, completing the construction shown in the figure we have, **if** $P'L = y$,

$$y^2 = x^2 + a^2,$$

and the elementary rectangle

$$P'M = \sqrt{x^2 + a^2}\, dx\,;$$

so that the area CA′K′N, in which CN = x_1

$$= \int^x \sqrt{x^2 + a^2}\, dx,$$

involving also a new integral, but nearer in form (note the limits of the integration) to what we obtained in the case of the circle and the ellipse.

We still refrain from the work of integration because we know from a familiar property of the hyperbola that there is yet another way of dealing with the curve which will probably give us the area more readily, and therefore show us how to integrate

$$\sqrt{x^2 - a^2}\, dx \text{ and } \sqrt{x^2 + a^2}\, dx$$

without our being at the pains to deal directly with these after any of the tentative methods yet described.

Take the rectangular hyperbola RAK, Fig. 22, with CZ and CZ′, the asymptotes, for the axes of reference. Draw CAS, the axis, and AG, PL, QM (near to PL), KN, all perpendicular to CZ.

Then CA = a and CG = $\sqrt{2}a = a_1$ (for convenience). Also, let CL = x, CM = $x + dx$,[1]

---

[1] We do not any longer write Δx and afterwards change to dx, but the reader will, of course, understand that dx is not really a finite increment, like LM, but is what this increment becomes as QM, in its approach to PL, is just about to merge into PL.

$CN = x_2$ (to distinguish **from** the x_1 of our former inquiry). Then, if $PL = y$, we know that, drawing

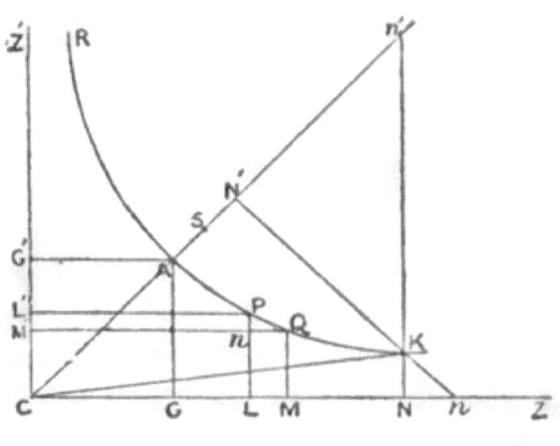

FIG. 22.

PL' and AG' perpendicular to CZ', rectangle L'L = square GG' = a_1^2 ; *i.e.*

$$xy = \frac{a^2}{2}.$$

Hence

$$y = \frac{a^2}{2x}.$$

Thus, the elementary rect. $QL = \dfrac{a^2}{2x} dx$,

and the area GAKN

$$= \int_{a_1}^{x_2} \frac{a^2}{2x} dx = \frac{a^2}{2} \left[\log x_2 - \log a_1 \right]$$

$$= \frac{a^2}{2} \log \frac{x_2}{a_1}.$$

Now draw KN' perpendicular to CAS, and put

$CN' = x_1$.   **Also join** CK.   **Then** we note that $\triangle CNK = \triangle CGA$; so that, taking each in succession from the area CAKN, we **have, area CAK** = area AGNK (which we have just determined).

Now area $APKN' = \triangle CN'K -$ area CAK; therefore we now have the area APKN' in the toils. For

$$\triangle CN'K = \tfrac{1}{2}CN' \cdot N'K = \tfrac{1}{2}x_1\sqrt{x_1^2 - a^2}$$

$$\text{Area } CAK = \text{area } GAKN = \frac{a^2}{2} \log \frac{CN}{CG}.$$

But if we draw NKn', N'Kn, as **in the figure, we** know that

$$CN = Nn' = \frac{Cn}{\sqrt{2}}.$$

So that

$$\frac{CN}{CG} = \frac{Cn'}{\sqrt{2}CG} = \frac{Cn'}{CA} = \frac{CN' + N'n'}{a}$$

$$= \frac{CN' + N'K}{a} = \frac{x_1 + \sqrt{x_2^2 - a^2}}{a}.$$

Wherefore, area **APKN'**

$$= \frac{1}{2}x_1\sqrt{x_1^2 - a^2} - \frac{a^2}{2} \log \frac{x_1 + \sqrt{x_1^2 - a^2}}{a}.$$

In the next lesson I **shall show how we have** thus ascertained the integral **of both**

$$\sqrt{x^2 - a^2} \text{ and } \sqrt{x^2 + a^2}$$

LESSON XX.

SUBSIDIARY INTEGRALS.

IN our last we found the area we first set out to find—viz. APKN (in Fig. 23)—by an application of

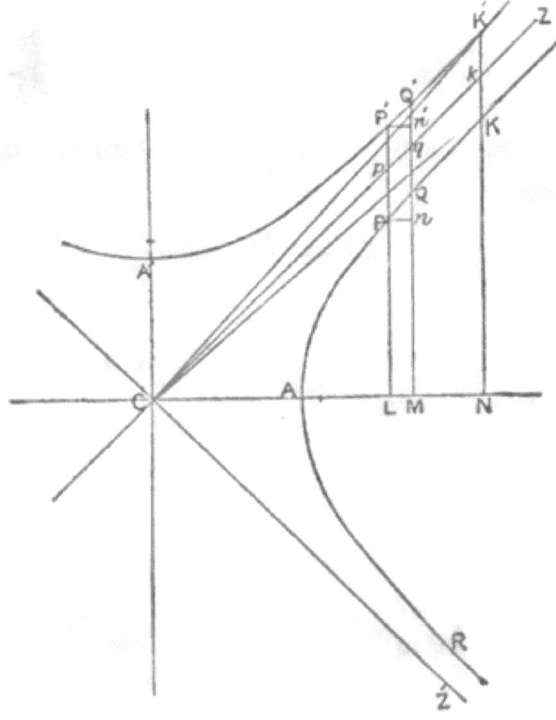

FIG. 23.

the integral calculus; though we should have failed if we had not known that

$$\int \frac{dx}{x} = \log x,$$

and therefore if we had not first had the particular function called a logarithm invented for us, and its qualities, value, and so forth, ascertained.

But we want also, now, to learn what is the

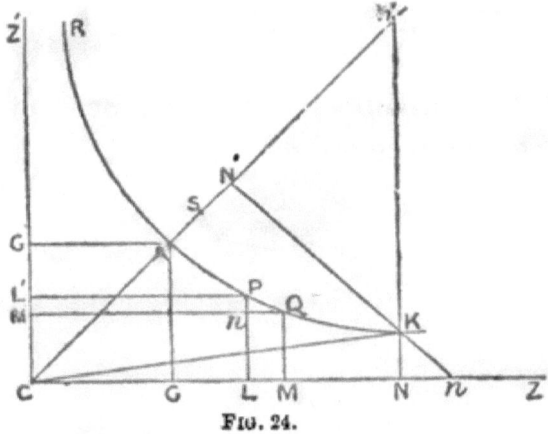

Fig. 24.

integral of $\sqrt{x^2 - a^2}\, dx$. We can form a pretty shrewd guess from the value we have already obtained for the area APKN′ (Fig. 24). If we write x for x_1 in that expression, and differentiate with respect to x, we find that that expression *is* the integral we want. However, it is better to work it out properly. And noting its resemblance in form to the integral of $\sqrt{a^2 - x^2}$ we are led naturally to deal with it in the same way. It would, in fact, be obviously the correct thing at this stage to see if the short method given for finding that integral may not be applied directly to this one. Let us see. Integrating by parts

$$\int \sqrt{x^2 - a^2}\, dx = x\sqrt{x^2 - a^2} - \int \frac{x^2 dx}{\sqrt{x^2 - a^2}}$$

Also

$$\int \sqrt{x^2 - a^2}\, dx = \int \frac{(x^2 - a^2)dx}{\sqrt{x^2 - a^2}} = \int \frac{x^2 dx}{\sqrt{x^2 - a^2}} - \int \frac{a^2 dx}{\sqrt{x^2 - a^2}}$$

∴ adding,

$$2\int \sqrt{x^2 - a^2}\, dx = x\sqrt{x^2 - a^2} - \int \frac{a^2 dx}{\sqrt{x^2 - a^2}} \quad (1)$$

Here we find ourselves stopped for want of knowledge as to the integral of

$$\frac{dx}{\sqrt{x^2 - a^2}}.$$

In the other case we had, instead,

$$\frac{dx}{\sqrt{a^2 - x^2}},$$

and we knew the integral of this to be

$$\sin^{-1}\left(\frac{x}{a}\right);$$

but we have not yet determined the integral of

$$\frac{dx}{\sqrt{x^2 - a^2}}.$$

How shall we set to work to find it? Manifestly our proper course is to take advantage of what we have already learned—viz. that the **part of** the integral we yet have to find involves

$$x + \sqrt{x^2 - a^2}.$$

This suggests **our** adopting **the** method of substitution and putting

$$x + \sqrt{x^2 - a^2} = z,$$

that is

$$\sqrt{x^2 - a^2} = z - x.$$

Then

$$x^2 - a^2 = z^2 - 2xz + x^2; \text{ or } 2xz - z^2 = a^2.$$

Whence, differentiating $2xz + x^2$ with respect to z,

$$2x + 2z \frac{dx}{dz} - 2z = 0,$$

or

$$\frac{dx}{dz} = \frac{z - x}{z}.$$

Hence we have

$$\int \frac{dx}{\sqrt{x^2 - a^2}} = \int \frac{1}{z - x} \cdot \frac{dx}{dz} \cdot dz = \int \frac{dz}{z}$$
$$= \log z = \log (x + \sqrt{x^2 - a^2}),$$

and thus we are able to complete the desired integration of (1), and obtain

$$\int \sqrt{x^2 - a^2}\, dx = \frac{x\sqrt{x^2 - a^2}}{2} - \frac{a^2}{2} \log (x + \sqrt{x^2 - a^2}.$$

It will be found that

$$\frac{1}{\sqrt{x^2 + a^2}} \text{ and } \sqrt{x^2 + a^2}$$

may be similarly integrated, with the results indicated on the next page.

LESSON XXI.

SUBSIDIARY INTEGRALS (*continued*).

COLLECTING the results we have obtained in the last
two lessons, so far as they add to the number of our
known integrals, we have

$$\int \sqrt{a^2 - x^2}\, dx = \frac{x\sqrt{x^2 - a^2}}{2} - \frac{a^2}{2}\sin^{-1}\frac{x}{a}$$

$$\int \sqrt{x^2 - a^2}\, dx = \frac{x\sqrt{a^2 - a^2}}{2} - \frac{a^2}{2}\log\left(x + \sqrt{x^2 - a^2}\right)$$

$$\int \sqrt{x^2 + a^2}\, dx = \frac{x\sqrt{x^2 - a^2}}{2} + \frac{a^2}{2}\log\left(x + \sqrt{x^2 + a^2}\right)$$

$$\int \frac{dx}{\sqrt{x^2 - a^2}} = \log\left(x + \sqrt{x^2 - a^2}\right)$$

$$\int \frac{dx}{\sqrt{x^2 + a^2}} = \log\left(x + \sqrt{x^2 + a^2}\right).$$

These results should be committed to memory,
because these logarithms are of frequent occurrence.
As for the first, it is easily remembered from the
relation which, as already pointed out, it bears to a
circular area. The next two are similarly related to
the areas APKN and CA'K'N in Fig. 22. Also, if
AK, AK' be joined, it will be seen how the first

part of the one represents the triangle CKN, while the first part of the other represents the triangle CK′N—the logarithmic parts representing respectively the areas APKC and A′P′K′C. These areas, then, are represented by the fourth and fifth of the above tabulated integrals.

It seems natural to inquire whether the curved surfaces, ACK, A′CK′, Fig. 23, can be so readily shown to be represented by the fourth and fifth integrals, that a convenient aid to the memory may be obtained from the relation. We shall not find this to be the case; but we shall be led in the course of the inquiry to notice a few more integrals important enough to be added to those we have already obtained.

Obviously, the only way to get the areas ACK and A′CK′ is to proceed by polar formulæ. Thus, let APQK, Fig. 25, be part of a rectangular hyperbola, C the centre, CA the axis. Then we know[1] that if CP $= r$, and ACP $= \theta$

$$r^2 = \frac{a^2}{\cos^2 \theta - \sin^2 \theta} = \frac{a^2}{\cos 2\theta}.$$

Now, if PCQ $= d\theta$, we have,

elementary area PCQ $= \dfrac{r^2}{2} \cdot d\theta = \dfrac{a^2 d\theta}{2 \cos 2\theta}$,

---

[1] We give, in fact, the well-known polar equation of the rectangular hyperbola; but it can be deduced at once from the relation already given, $y^2 = x^2 - a^2$, by putting $y = r \sin \theta$, and $x = r \cos \theta$.

and if $KCA = a$, we have

$$\text{area } APKC = \frac{a^2}{2} \int_0^a \frac{d\theta}{\cos 2\theta}.$$

Thus to integrate

$$\int \frac{d\theta}{\cos 2\theta} \text{ and } \int \frac{d\theta}{\sin 2\theta}$$

is our next care.

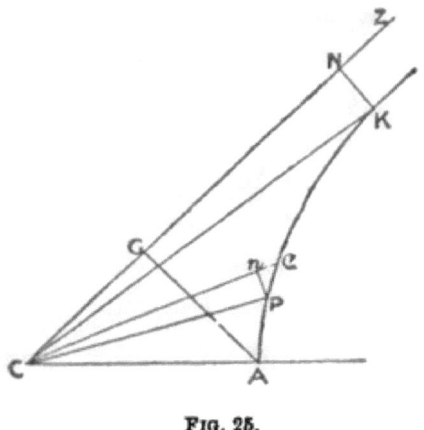

FIG. 25.

Take the second first, as more likely to be easy. We have

$$\int \frac{d\theta}{\sin 2\theta} = \int \frac{d\theta}{2 \sin \theta \cos \theta} = \int \frac{\cos \theta d\theta}{2 \sin \theta \cos^2 \theta}$$

$$= \tfrac{1}{2} \int \frac{1}{\tan \theta} \cdot \frac{d \tan \theta}{d\theta} \cdot d\theta = \tfrac{1}{2} \log \tan \theta.$$

Whence we obtain

$$\int \frac{d\theta}{\cos 2\theta}$$

very easily : for

$$\text{Put } \theta = \frac{\pi}{4} - \phi; \text{ so that } \frac{d\theta}{d\phi} = -1.$$

Then

$$\int \frac{d\theta}{\cos 2\theta} = \int \frac{1}{\sin 2\phi} \cdot \frac{d\theta}{d\phi} \cdot d\phi = -\int \frac{d\phi}{\sin 2\phi}$$

$$= -\frac{1}{2} \log \tan \phi = -\frac{1}{2} \log \tan \left(\frac{\pi}{4} - \theta\right)$$

$$= \frac{1}{2} \log \cot \left(\frac{\pi}{4} - \theta\right).$$

Hence area APKC, Fig. 25,

$$= \frac{a^2}{4} \left[\log \cot \left(\frac{\pi}{4} - a\right)\right] \left(\because \log \cot \frac{\pi}{4} = 0\right)$$

$$= \frac{a^2}{4} \log \cot \text{ KCN}$$

$$= \frac{a^2}{4} \log \frac{\text{CN}}{\text{NK}}.$$

$$= \frac{a^2}{4} \log \frac{\text{CN}^2}{\text{CN} \cdot \text{NK}} \quad \text{or} = \frac{a^2}{4} \log \frac{\text{CN} \cdot \text{NK}}{(\text{NK})^2}$$

$$= \frac{a^2}{4} \log \frac{(\text{CN})^2}{(\text{CG})^2} \quad \text{or} = \frac{a^2}{4} \log \frac{(\text{AG})^2}{(\text{NK})^2}$$

$$= \frac{a^2}{2} \log \frac{\text{CN}}{\text{CG}} \quad \text{or} = \frac{a^2}{2} \log \frac{\text{AG}}{\text{NK}}.$$

We have seen already that AQKC, Fig. 25, =GAKN. Hence the result just obtained shows that we may write—

$$\text{Area GAKN} = \frac{a^2}{2} \log \frac{x_1}{a_1} \quad \text{or} = \frac{a^2}{2} \log \frac{a_1}{y_1}$$

I

(putting $NK = y_1$). This is, of course, obvious, since $a_1^2 = x_1 y_1$, that is,

$$\frac{a_1}{y_1} = \frac{x_1}{a_1}.$$

But it is convenient to note the two forms.

Putting

$$a = \frac{\pi}{4},$$

or carrying the radius vector on to coincidence with the asymptote CZ, we find that the area between the asymptote, the semi-axis CA, and the curve AQK to infinity

$$= \frac{a^2}{2} \log (\cot 0) = \text{infinity.}$$

We may here add to our list of known integrals these :—

$$\int \frac{d\theta}{\sin \theta} = \log \tan \frac{\theta}{2} ; \quad \text{and} \int \frac{d\theta}{\cos \theta} = \log \cot \left(\frac{\pi}{4} - \frac{\theta}{2}\right)$$

$$\int \frac{d\theta}{\sin 2\theta} = \frac{1}{2} \log \tan \theta ; \quad \text{and} \int \frac{d\theta}{\cos 2\theta} = \frac{1}{2} \log \cot \left(\frac{\pi}{4} - \theta\right)$$

$$\int \frac{d\theta}{\sin n\theta} = \frac{1}{n} \log \tan \frac{n\theta}{2} ; \quad \text{and} \int \frac{d\theta}{\cos n\theta} = \frac{1}{n} \log \cot \left(\frac{\pi}{4} - \frac{n\theta}{2}\right) ;$$

making twenty-five integrals in all—with those already tabulated. Knowing these, the student can deal with a wide range of problems depending on integration.

Spottiswoode & Co. Printers, New-street Square, London.